# 就算不用考

# 英文

## 也要繼續

# speak English

**基本會話**　**搭訕起手式**

**求職用語**　**旅遊英文**

掌握這幾大類常用英語，
流利的對話比你想的還容易！

U0087387

# 目錄

前言

## 上篇　日常生活 Daily Life

### Chapter1　為人之道 Good Manners

Unit 1 客套禮節 Basic Etiquette ···················· 10

Unit 2 勿忘說聲謝謝 Saying Thanks ················· 15

Unit 3 委婉邀請別人 Euphemistic Invitation ········ 21

Unit 4 與人搭訕 Talking with Strangers ············· 26

Unit 5 朋友多，路好走 Making Friends ············· 33

### Chapter2　出行求助 Nice Trip

Unit 1 向別人問路 Asking the Way ················· 39

Unit 2 如何乘車 How to Take a Bus or Subway ······ 43

Unit 3 火車站諮詢 Train Station ··················· 49

Unit 4 機場協助一瞥 Airport Situation ············· 54

### Chapter3　日常瑣事 Daily Matters

Unit 1 求租房屋 House Hunting ···················· 59

Unit 2 求醫問藥 Seeing a Doctor ·················· 65

Unit 3 電話求助 Calling for Help ·················· 71

Unit 4 處理投訴 Dealing with Complaints ··········· 77

# 目錄

## Chapter4　公務事宜 Public Affairs

Unit 1 綠色郵政 Post Office ·····················83

Unit 2 退換商品 Exchanging and Refunding ··············89

Unit 3 詢問匯率與利率 Inquiring about Exchange and Interest Rates····94

Unit 4 兌換外幣 Foreign Currency Exchange ············· 101

## Chapter5　人在旅途 On the Way

Unit 1 旅遊諮詢 Making Sightseeing Enquiries ············· 108

Unit 2 賓館接待 At the Reception Desk ···············112

Unit 3 觀光遊覽 Do Some Sightseeing ···············119

Unit 4 文化交流 Culture Exchange ···············128

## 下篇　職場社交 Business and Social Life

## Chapter1　暢通求職 Smooth Job-hunting

Unit 1 打點好你自己 Dressing Up Well ·············· 138

Unit 2 職位諮詢 Enquiry about the Job Vacancy ·········· 144

Unit 3 應徵求職 Job-hunting Interview ·············· 149

Unit 4 請多指教 Working for the First Day ············· 155

Unit 5 搞好同事關係 Co-workers' Relationship ··········· 161

## Chapter2　工作交際 Office Situation

Unit 1 要求加薪 Paying a Rise ················ 167

Unit 2 申請升職 Applying for Promotion ············· 172

Unit 3 向老闆請假 Asking for a Leave ············· 178

Unit 4 接待工作 Reception Service ················· 182

Unit 5 電話找人 Call in Someone ················· 189

Unit 6 留個口信 Leaving a Message ················· 195

## Chapter3　公事公辦 Business Time

Unit 1 預約見面 Making an Appointment ················· 201

Unit 2 有事拜訪 Paying a Visit ················· 206

Unit 3 電話推銷 Promotion By Telephone ················· 211

Unit 4 建立合作關係 Establishing Trade Relations ················· 217

Unit 5 銷售談判 Negotiation by Salesperson ················· 222

Unit 6 砍價折扣交易 Mark-down and Discount ················· 232

## Chapter4　社交門道 Social Courtesy

Unit 1 贈送禮物 Sending Gifts ················· 239

Unit 2 請客吃飯 My Treat ················· 245

Unit 3 懂得適時讚美 Compliment People ················· 252

Unit 4 請人幫忙 Asking for Help ················· 257

# 目錄 ─────────────────────────

# 前言

　　世上沒有做不到的事，只有不會做事的人。一個會做事的人，可以在紛繁複雜的環境裡輕鬆自如地駕馭人生局面，凡事逢凶化吉，把不可能的事變成可能，最後達到自己的目的。其中的關鍵是看你用什麼方法、用什麼技巧、用什麼手段。

　　語言是交流的重要工具，學英文若光學不練，則無異於「紙上談兵」，只有切身體驗、即時運用，才會學到英文的真經。日常生活中，求人做事是常發生的事，那麼如何用英文來求人做事，這裡特地為你奉上這本實用有效的英文學習書。

　　這本道地口語書從「日常生活」與「職場社交」入手，用英文的思維、禮節與方法，向你娓娓道來求人做事裡點點滴滴的細節。我們知道中西方存在著巨大的文化差異，所以，外國人的說話方式、行為方式、禮節方式就跟我們有各自不同的特點，若我們照自己的思考方式去說和做，在與外國人的交流中必敗無疑。

　　因此，在與老外和諧共處、建立關係、求其做事，必須要有一套自己的英文口語法則。而本書就是要為你量身打造這種法則，以期讓你用英文自如地與老外閒談、商談，達到彼此的雙贏。

　　本書集實用性、即時性、多樣性、豐富性、文化性於一身，精選對話，精粹句型。

　　用心去學、用腦去做，就沒有做不到的事情，無論大事小事，相信你都可以應對自如。

編者

# 目錄

# 上篇
# 日常生活 Daily Life

## Chapter1
# 為人之道 Good Manners

## Unit 1 客套禮節 Basic Etiquette

### Fresh Expressions

I've heard so much about you.

久仰，久仰。

I didn't expect to meet you here.

沒想到在這裡遇見你。

Hi, Tom, I'm glad I bumped into you.

嗨，湯姆，很高興遇見你。

What a pleasant surprise! I haven't seen you for a long time.

真叫人驚喜！我好久沒看到你了。

What have you been up to these days?

你最近在做些什麼？

Please allow me to introduce you to my friends present.

請允許我把你介紹給在場的朋友們。

John, I'd like to meet my friend, Daniel.

約翰，來認識一下我的朋友丹尼爾。

I have been looking forward to seeing you.

一直都盼望見到您。

I've wanted to meet you for a long time.

我早就想認識你了。

Thank you for introducing me to such a very nice person.

謝謝您介紹那麼好的人給我認識。

Ladies and gentlemen, it is a great honor for us to have Mr. Smith here.

女士們及先生們，我們很榮幸請到了史密斯先生。

This is Mr. Wang, he is working as an assistant manager in the Sale Department.

這位是王先生，銷售部副經理。

## Interactive Dialogues

### Dialogue 1

A：Excuse me, are you Mr. Brown from US?

A：對不起，您是從美國來的布朗先生嗎？

B：Yes, I am.

B：是的。

A：How do you do? I'm Wang from Taipei. Welcome to Taiwan!

A：你好，布朗先生。我是臺北的王先生，歡迎您來臺灣！

B：Thank you. It's a pleasure to have the opportunity to visit Taiwan.

B：謝謝。有機會訪問臺灣我感到高興。

A：The pleasure's all ours. We have been looking forward to meeting you.

A：我們感到非常榮幸。我們一直盼望見到您。

B：I'm afraid this must be a lot of trouble for you.

B：恐怕這一定會給你們添很多麻煩。

A：No, no trouble at all. Well, I think you must be tired after such a long trip.

A：沒關係。我想這麼長的旅途，您一定累了。

B：Oh, no, I am not tired at all. The service on the plane was excellent and I had a very pleasant journey.

B：不，我一點也不累。機上服務非常好，旅途很愉快。

A：I'm glad to hear that. Mr. Brown, shall we go to the waiting-room for a short rest before going through the formalities?

A：那太好了。布朗先生，在辦理手續前我們先去休息室休息一下好嗎？

B：That's a good idea.

B：好主意。

### Notes

- hello 和 how do you do 用法上沒有太大的差別，都可以用來打招呼。如果要深究，hello 比較隨意一點，而 how do you do 一般用於比較正式的場合，如甲向乙介紹丙，乙就可以說 how do you do，而不用 hello。

- It's pleasure to do sth. 做……感到高興或榮幸。而 It's a pleasure. 這句話常用作別人向你表示致謝時的答語，意思是「別客氣」，此時相當於 My pleasure./It's My pleasure. With pleasure 通常是表示願意接受對方的建議。如果對方請你幫忙，你很樂意，就可以說 With pleasure.。

- look forward to 意為「盼望」。這裡的「to」不是動詞不定式的標誌，而是一個介詞。所以當你想要表達「盼望見到某人」這個動作時，應該把這個動詞轉換成動名詞的形式。比如，當我們表達「盼望見到某人」時，我們應該說成「look forward to meeting/seeing sb.」而絕對不能寫成「look forward to meet/see sb.」。如果盼望的是一件事情時，我們就可以直接在介詞 to 的後面用名詞形式。

Dialogue 2

A：Good afternoon.

A：午安。

B：Good afternoon, what can I do for you?

B：午安。我能為你做些什麼？

A：Yes. My name is Daisy Darrow. This is my card. Does Royce live here?

A：我叫黛西·達羅。這是我的名片。羅伊斯住在這裡嗎？

B：That's my father. I am Lydia. Come on in, Ms. Darrow. Dad, Ms. Darrow is here to meet you.

B：他是我父親。我叫莉迪亞。達羅女士，請進。爸爸，達羅女士來見你了。

A：Just a moment, please.

A：請稍等一會兒。

B：Would you like something to drink, Ms. Darrow? Do you prefer tea or coffee?

B：想喝點什麼嗎，達羅女士？茶還是咖啡？

A：Tea, please. Thank you.

A：請給我茶。謝謝。

B：Here you are, Ms. Darrow.

B：請喝茶，達羅女士。

C：Hello, Ms. Darrow. It's a surprise to see you. How are you?

C：你好，達羅女士。真沒想到會見到妳。妳好嗎？

A：Very nice. You are as strong as ten years ago.

A：很好。你還是跟 10 年前一樣強壯。

C：Everything is going well with me. I hope you can be here for quite a few days.

C：我一切都好。希望妳能在這裡多待幾天。

A：Unfortunately, I have to leave this afternoon. I'm here between trains.

A：遺憾的是，我今天下午就要離開。我是趁轉火車的間隔時間來這裡的。

B：What a pity!

B：真是太遺憾了！

**Notes**

■ come on in 與 come in 在意思上是一致的。在 come 和 in 之間加 on，是一種語意態度上的強化，更加隨和、友好。

Come on in 北美國家非常常用。意為：（來，快請）進來吧！

相關的說法：come on out; come (on) over here.

■ Just a moment, please. 或者「Just a second, please.」都表示「稍等一下」的意思。此外與「moment」有關的詞組還有：

・ for a moment ＝ for a while 表示一個動作持續了「一下子」。例如：

　　—— Have you ever thought of that?

　　你想過那件事嗎？

　　—— Not for a moment.

　　從來沒有。

・ for the moment 目前；暫時。例如：

　　I have no enough money for the moment.

　　目前我沒有足夠的錢。

・ in a moment 立即；馬上；一下子。例如：

The film will start in a moment.

電影馬上就要開演了。

· at the moment 此刻；當時。例如：

I'm afraid I'm too busy at the moment to see anyone.

很遺憾，我此刻太忙，不能去見任何人。

· at any moment 意為「隨時」。例如：

He told me I could call him at any moment.

他告訴我隨時可以打電話給他。

此外，the moment ＋句子，相當於 as soon as「一……就……」。此時可用 the minute；the instant；the second 等替代。例如：

I'll tell him the news the moment he comes.

他一來我就告訴他這個消息。

■ everything is going well with sb. 某人一切都好。例如：

I hope everything is going well with you.

我希望你諸事如意。

■ between trains 轉乘火車的間隔時間

# Unit 2 勿忘說聲謝謝 Saying Thanks

## Fresh Expressions

Thanks a million for your generous gift.

你慷慨地送我禮物，真是太感謝了。

Thank you for your kindness to Dick during his illness.

謝謝你在迪克生病期間為他所做的一切。

It's so kind of you to send us a gift.

你真的太好了，還送我們禮物。

I really appreciate your help.

我真的很感謝你的幫助。

We all appreciate your kind support.

我們都很感謝你友好的支持。

It's very considerate of you to do so.

你這麼做真是太體貼了。

It's so thoughtful of you to give me such valuable advice.

你給我如此寶貴的建議,考慮得實在太周到了。

A thousand thanks for your friendly advice.

對你善意的建議,我表示萬分感謝。

Many thanks for your remembering my birthday.

你還記得我的生日,真是太感謝了。

We will never forget what you did for us.

我們永遠也忘不了你的幫助。

I don't know what I would do without you.

我不知道沒有你我該怎麼做。

## Interactive Dialogues

### Dialogue 1

A：Hello.

A：您好。

B：Oh, hello, Bobby. How are you doing these days?

B：哦,您好,鮑比。近來好嗎?

A：I'm much better, thank you very much. I was just about to call to tell you how I appreciate the flowers you sent me.

A：好多了，謝謝您。我正要打電話告訴您，您送的花我真是太喜歡了。

B：I'm glad you like them, Bobby. Your wife said yellow roses are your favorite.

B：我很高興您喜歡，鮑比。您太太說您喜歡黃玫瑰。

A：Yes, they're really beautiful. Thank you very much.

A：是的，黃玫瑰真的很美。太感謝了。

B：That's my pleasure, Bobby. Just hope you're feeling better.

B：不用謝，鮑比。我多希望您好起來。

A：I am. The doctor says I can go home the day after tomorrow.

A：我是好起來了。醫生說我後天就能出院了。

B：Day after tomorrow —— so soon —— wow, Bobby, that's marvelous. I bet Celia was very happy to hear that.

B：後天 —— 這麼快 —— 哇！鮑比，太棒了。我想西莉亞聽到這個好消息一定很高興。

A：She doesn't know it yet. I found out only an hour ago. I couldn't have reached her so soon.

A：她還不知道呢。我也是一小時前才知道的。我還沒來得及那麼快告訴她。

B：She'll be so pleased when you tell her. Peter was just talking to her and she said she was getting ready to drive over to see you.

B：當您告訴她時，她一定會很高興的。剛才彼得跟她交談過，她還說要驅車前來看你呢。

A：When did she say that?

17

A：她什麼時候說的？

B：Oh, about half an hour ago. She'd be there at the hospital any time now.

B：嗯，大約半小時前。現在她隨時都可能到。

A：Here she is now. She's walking toward the room.

A：她來了。正往這邊走來呢。

B：Bobby, if Celia's here, you go ahead and tell her the good news. I'll hang up and we can talk later.

B：鮑比，既然西莉亞來了，那就告訴她這個好消息。那我就掛了，我們以後再聊。

A：Dajiang, before you hang up. I want to tell you again how much I love the flowers.

A：大江，在您掛斷之前，我還想再次告訴您，我真的非常喜歡這些花。

B：Well, you know it gave me a lot of pleasure to send them to you. Now tell her your news and I'll be seeing you when you're home. Bye.

B：嗯，您知道的，送花給您也讓我感到無比快樂。現在把好消息告訴她。等你回家後，我再去看您。再見。

A：Bye.

A：再見。

**Notes**

■ 問候對方家人的近況，是禮貌和表示親近的做法，最常見的句型是以「How is (are)…」開頭的問句。「How is (someone) doing?」並非詢問「某人做得如何？」而是「近來可好？」的意思，這是美式口語的慣

用法。像「How're you doing?」就是問「你好嗎？」

■ be about to 表示即將、馬上要做某事。例如：

We were about to set out when it began to rain.

我們正要動身，就在這時開始下雨了。

■ drive over 意為「開車前往」。

## Dialogue 2

A：All my bags are checked in. I guess I'm all set to go.

A：我的行李都送進去了。我想都沒問題了。

B：I know you must be excited to go home after such a long business trip.

B：出差這麼久，終於要回家了，我想妳一定很高興。

A：I am sure. It's always good to work with you, Tom. I really appreciate all of your hospitality.

A：那當然。湯姆，和你們合作總是很愉快。我真的很感謝你的招待。

B：It was my pleasure. And I'd like to give you a little something to take home. Let me unroll it.

B：我很榮幸。而且我有樣小東西想給你帶回家。讓我把它打開。

A：This is beautiful! Chinese calligraphy. That's very nice of you. Where did you get it? It's not a print.

A：真漂亮！是中華書法。你真好。你從哪裡獲得的？這還不是複製品。

B：No, it's an original. My father's friend is a calligrapher, and I had him make it for you. His name and the date are on the bottom.

B：沒錯，這可是真跡。我父親的朋友是書法家，所以我請他寫一幅給你。他的名字和日期都在下面。

A：I'll hang it in my office. But I feel bad I didn't get you anything.

A：我會把它掛在辦公室。不過，真不好意思，我什麼也沒送你。

B：Don't worry about it. It's a token of my appreciation for your business and friendship.

B：別放在心上！這是表示我們在生意及友誼上的一點意思。

A：If you have time around Christmas, please come to visit my family. I'll be able to show you around our city.

A：如果你聖誕節前後有空，歡迎來我家玩。我可以帶你在我們城市四處看看。

B：Thanks for the invitation. And please give my regards to your wife.

B：謝謝你的邀請。請代我問候你夫人。

A：You do the same. Well, I'd better go. Thanks again for everything.

A：也代我問候你夫人。嗯，我得走了。再次謝謝你們的招待。

B：Take care, and have a nice flight.

B：請保重，祝你一路順風。

## Notes

- be all set 準備就緒。set 當形容詞，原本就有「準備好」之意；all set 是比較口語的用法。這個詞組即等於「be ready」，意指「一切都準備妥當，沒有問題了」，後面可接 to do sth. 表示準備好去做某事。

- a token of one's appreciation 代表感謝心意，這是一個經常在饋贈禮物時對收受者所說的話。token 是指代表某事物的「象徵」；「appreciation」意為「感激」。若是送東西給親密的朋友以表情意，就可說「This is a token of my love.」。

- give one's regards to 是固定搭配，意為「向……表示問候」。在此詞組中一定要用複數「regards」，指「請安、問候」之意。與此相同意思的搭配有：best wishes/regards to、give one's best wishes to sb.、give one's best love to sb.。

  無論在東西方，友人前往遠方時，通常都會說「一路平安」、「旅途愉快」等話。

- 「Take care.」是一般話別時所用的口頭語，即「保重」。「have a nice flight/trip」就是祝人「旅途愉快」。nice 是「愉快的」，可用「pleasant」、「good」等類似意思的字代替。

# Unit 3 委婉邀請別人 Euphemistic Invitation

## Fresh Expressions

Would you be interested in coming to the cinema with me tonight?

你今晚有興趣一起去看電影嗎？

We should be very delighted if you were able to come and have dinner with us.

如果您能來和我們共進晚餐，我們會很高興。

May we have the honor of having you as our guest of honor?

您能否賞光做我們的嘉賓？

Would you and your wife care to come to my home and have coffee with me tomorrow night?

你和你夫人有沒有空明晚來我家一起喝杯咖啡？

I should be honored if you were able to come to the banquet.

若您能參加這個宴會我會很榮幸的。

I'm phoning because I want to invite you to a party at our new house.

我打電話是因為我想請你到我們的新家來參加聚會。

It's very kind of you to invite me.

你能邀請我真是太好了。

Thank you. I'll be glad to come.

謝謝你。我很高興能來。

Could you make it another time, perhaps next Sunday?

你能改個時間嗎？下個星期天怎麼樣？

I'm sorry I can't, but thank you all the time.

真抱歉我去不了，不過還是很感謝你。

## Interactive Dialogues

### Dialogue 1

A：Hello, Mr. Gaul. How are you?

A：喂，Gaul 先生，你好嗎？

B：Hello, Ms. Wang. I'm fine, and you?

B：喂，王小姐，我很好，妳呢？

A：I'm doing fine, too. Well, Mr. Gaul, we are planning to have a casual get-together, and I wonder if you and Mrs. Gaul can join us.

A：我也很好。嗯，Gaul 先生，我們打算大家小聚一番，不知道你和夫人能不能賞光？

B：That sounds very nice. When will it be?

B：聽起來真不錯。什麼時候呢？

A：It's two weeks from this Wednesday.

A：下下個星期三。

B：What a pity! We have a previous engagement that day. How I wish we could come!

B：太可惜了！我們那天有約了。真希望我們能去！

A：Don't worry. Let's wait until the next time.

A：沒關係，下次還有機會。

**Notes**

- have a (casual) get-together 小聚一番。get-together 是從 get together 演變而來，本指「聚集」，這裡當名詞，意為「聚會」，例如聚餐、宴會等，為口語用法。casual 是「非正式的」，意指輕鬆小聚，異於正式的宴會。

- 英文中下個星期三，可說成 next Wednesday，但超過一個星期，如兩個星期或三個星期後的日期，就要用「…（時間）from…（日期）」的句型來表示。如對話中的 two weeks from this Wednesday。
pity 除了有「可憐」的涵義外，尚有「可惜的事；憾事」的意思。What a pity! 這句話的意思等於 What a shame!

- We are planning…, and I wonder if…can join us. 的句型是邀約他人的實用句；前半句解釋邀請活動的類型，後半句正式向對方提出邀約。wonder if 的意思是「不知道是否能……」，可用於請求，語氣十分客氣。

Dialogue 2

A：Hello, Miss Mary. How nice to see you again. Come in, please.

A：你好，瑪麗小姐。再次見到妳真是太好了。請進。

B：How fresh you are looking! I think that you must have had a refreshing sleep.

B：您看起來精神很好！我想您一定是好好地睡了一覺。

A：Yes, thank you.

A：是的，謝謝。

B：How do you think about the room service and the food here?

B：您覺得這家飯店的客房服務和食物如何？

A：The room service is quite satisfactory and the food very delicious. This is a very good hotel. I think they understand how difficult it is for a foreigner to be on business abroad.

A：客房服務非常令人滿意，食物也很可口。這是一家很不錯的飯店。我想他們真能體諒一名外國人在異國他鄉出差的困難。

B：I'm very happy to hear that. After all, it's your first trip here and we'd like you to feel at home.

B：聽您這麼說，我非常高興。畢竟這是您第一次來這裡，我們想讓您感覺就像在家一樣。

A：It is considerate of you, Miss Mary. Thank you for the trouble you've taken.

A：瑪麗小姐，妳考慮得真周到。勞妳費心了。

B：No trouble at all. Well, by the way, I wonder if you're free tonight?

B：沒什麼費心的。嗯，想順便問一下，您今晚有空嗎？

A：I'm not sure, but let me check my schedule. Ah, no, I have nothing on tonight.

A：我不確定，但讓我查一下行程表。嗯，沒有，今晚我沒有任何安排。

B：Great! Mr. Dickens has asked me to come over to invite you to the banquet held in your honor at the Shangri-La Hotel at 7:00 this evening. Here's an invitation for you.

B：太好了！迪肯斯先生要我來此請您參加今晚 7 點在香格里拉飯店為您舉行的宴會。這是給您的請束。

A：How nice of him. I'll be delighted to go. But what time would be convenient?

A：迪肯斯先生太客氣了。我很高興參加。但什麼時間點比較方便呢？

B：If you could be ready at 6:30 o'clock, I'll be at the hotel to pick you up.

B：如果您能在 6 點 30 分準備好，到時我來飯店接您。

A：That's good. It's most thoughtful of you to do this, Miss Mary.

A：好的。瑪麗小姐，妳想得可真周到。

B：It's my pleasure. Well, then, I'll say good-bye.

B：樂意效勞，那麼就再見啦。

A：Goodbye and see you tonight, Miss Mary.

A：再見，瑪麗小姐，今晚見。

## Notes

- have a refreshing sleep 意為「睡得很香」、「好好地睡一覺」。
- How do you think about... 特殊疑問詞＋ do you think（或其他表示心裡活動的詞）＋陳述語序。例如：
  - What should I do first? → What do you think I should do first?
    （被插入的疑問句原來為倒裝語序，插入後成為陳述語序）
  - Who is singing? → Who do you think is singing?
    （被插入的疑問句原來就是陳述語序，不需要做調整）
- in one's honor 意為「為紀念；為慶祝……；向……表示敬意」。

- 詞組 pick up 本意是「拾起」、「收拾」，在 pick sb. up or pick up sb. 詞組中，解釋為「接某人」。例如：

Shall I pick you up at the hotel?

我到飯店接你好嗎？

- 對話中的 It is considerate of you. 與 It's most thoughtful of you to do this. 這兩句話，都是用來表示「你想得很周到」之意。

# Unit 4 與人搭訕 Talking with Strangers

## Fresh Expressions

You look like someone I know.

你跟我一個朋友長得好像。

Haven't we met before?

我們之前見過吧？

Wow, where did you pick up your Chinese? You speak Chinese so well!

哇！你在哪裡學中文的？你中文講得好棒呀！

Are you interested in doing a language exchange with me?

你有興趣和我做語言交流嗎？

We can have lunch or a tea break together next time.

我們下次可以一起吃個午餐或喝個下午茶。

Your bus is coming. It's Route A Bus and I have to take Route B Bus. Before you get on the bus, let's exchange our numbers so we can hang out next time.

你的公車來了。那是 A 號車，我應該要搭 B 號車。在你上車前，我們交換一下電話，這樣我們下次就能碰面了。

## Interactive Dialogues

Dialogue 1

A：I believe you're Mr. Mailer, aren't you?

A：我想你是梅勒先生，對嗎？

B：Yeah, but how did you know?

B：沒錯，但你是怎麼知道的呢？

A：I attended your lecture about the sustainable development the other day. Your views impressed me deeply, and I like the way you delivered it.

A：我參加前幾天你的可持續性發展講座。你的觀點給我留下了很深的印象，我也非常喜歡你闡述問題的方式。

B：I'm very happy you like it. May I know your name?

B：我很高興你喜歡。請問你叫什麼名字？

A：I'm Merlin Senior.

A：我叫默林‧西尼爾。

B：Nice to meet you here, Mr. Senior. Why not sit down and have a cup of coffee with me? Hello, Mr. Waiter, serve Mr. Senior a cup of coffee.

B：很高興在這裡見到你，西尼爾先生。坐下來跟我喝杯咖啡好嗎？哈囉，服務生，請給西尼爾先生來一杯咖啡。

A：Thank you, Mr. Mailer.

A：多謝你，梅勒先生。

Notes

- the other day 不久前某一天

  one day（過去）某一天；（將來）有一天。例如：

  He'll come to realize it one day.

他總有一天會懂得這一點。

（將來）總有一天，（日後）某天。例如：

We will meet again some day.

後會有期。

■ why not 意思是「為什麼不呢？」，在很多電影裡經常聽到。一般用在疑問句中，表示提出建議。why not 後面要跟動詞原型。例如：

Why not have a picnic this afternoon?

今天下午去野餐怎麼樣？

why not ＝ why don't sb. 二者用法是完全一致的，可以相互轉化。例如：

Why not go out or a walk = Why don't we go out for a walk

何不出去散散步呢？

## Dialogue 2

A：Excuse me, is this seat taken?

A：對不起，這個座位有人嗎？

B：No. It's all yours.

B：沒有。是妳的了。

A：Thank you very much. My name is Ashley. It's nice to meet you.

A：非常感謝。我叫艾胥雷，很高興認識你。

B：Carson. Nice meeting you, too.

B：卡森。我也很高興認識妳。

A：The weather is so warm for December, don't you think?

A：這天氣對 12 月來說有點太暖和了，你覺得呢？

B：It's unusually warm. I believe it is because of global warming.

B：暖和到不正常了。我覺得這應該歸咎於地球暖化。

A：Global warming is wreaking havoc everywhere.

A：地球暖化引發了全球的大災難。

B：So sure. Are you from around here?

B：沒錯。妳是本地人嗎？

A：No, I'm new here. I just moved here a few months ago.

A：不是，我是新來的。幾個月前才剛搬來的。

B：Where are you from?

B：那妳是哪裡人？

A：I'm from Taiwan. What about you?

A：我來自臺灣，你呢？

B：I'm from Texas. I was in Taiwan once, but it was a long time ago.

B：我來自德克薩斯州。我以前去過一次臺灣，不過那是很久以前的事情了。

A：Did you enjoy it?

A：你喜歡哪裡嗎？

B：I did. I especially liked the food. What do you think about the food here?

B：很喜歡。尤其是喜歡那裡的食物。妳覺得這裡的食物如何？

A：It's very different from Chinese food, but I'm getting used to it.

A：跟中餐很不同，不過我正在慢慢適應。

B：Is that the Da Vinci Code that you've got there?

B：妳拿的是《達文西密碼》吧？

A：Yes. Have you read it?

A：對，你看過了嗎？

B：No, but I saw the movie. What do you think about it?

B：沒有，不過我看過電影。妳覺得寫得怎麼樣呢？

A：Well, to be honest, I've only gotten through 10 pages of it. So far, though, it's interesting.

A：嗯，老實說，我才剛看 10 頁。不過目前為止，還滿有意思的。

B：OK. This is my stop. It was nice talking with you.

B：好的。我到站了。跟妳聊天很開心。

A：Likewise, bye!

A：我也是，再見！

## Notes

■ Are you from around here? 這句是詢問別人「你是本地人嗎？」，這種說法常用在陌生人交談中。

■ 「很高興認識你」英文表達有：

It's nice/good to meet you.

Glad to know you.

It was a pleasure meeting you.

I'm very happy to meet you.

Nice to meet you./Nice meeting you.

Pleased to meet you.

It's nice/a pleasure meeting you!

■ 比較 though 與 although 的用法：

‧ 兩者同義並可換用，但 although 語氣較重，通常放在句首並用於正

式場合。如：

He'd quite like to go out, (al)though it is a bit late.

他很想外出，雖然為時稍晚。

Although it is winter, it is not very cold.

雖然是冬天了，但不是很冷。

- although 引導從句常指事實，而 though 引導的句子可表假設。如：

Let's start as arranged though it rains tomorrow.

即使明天下雨，我們也照預定的計畫出發吧！（假設）

I was not unhappy although I had to live alone.

雖然得一個人生活，我毫無不快之感。（事實）

- although 只用作連詞，而 though 除作連詞外，還可用作副詞，常置於句末。句子較長時，也置於句中。如：

It's hard work, he enjoys it though.

這是苦差事，但他樂在其中。

There's no excuse, though, for telling a lie to her.

對她說謊一事，還是不可原諒。

- 用 though 時，可將強調的詞前置，但 although 不能。as 也有此種倒裝結構。如：

Alone though/as he is, he is happy.

他雖然單獨生活，但很愉快。

Child though/as he was, he had to make a living.

儘管他還是個孩子，他必須自己去謀生。（child 前無冠詞 a）

- though 可用於 even though，as though 等結構；although 則不能。如：

Even though I fail, I'll keep on trying.

我縱然失敗，仍會繼續嘗試下去。

You look as though (= as if) you know each other.

看起來你們好像彼此認識。

- although 和 though 用作連詞時不能和 but 連用，但可跟 yet、still 等連用。如：

  Although he lives alone, yet he is happy.（= He lives alone, but he is happy.）

  雖然他獨自生活，但很愉快。

- though 常用於省略句。如：

  Though (he is) poor, he is happy.

  雖然他窮，但過得很愉快。

■ get used to 表示（變得）習慣於做某事，側重過程。例如：

The food here is not so tasty but you will get used to that.

這裡的食物不怎麼樣，但你會慢慢習慣的。

be used to 表示（已經）習慣於做某事，側重結果。例如：

Mary is used to her husband's bad temper.

Mary 習慣了她丈夫的壞脾氣。

■ it's nice doing sth. 做了某件事真好（事情已經做完了）

It's nice to do sth. 做某事真好（沒有做，即將要做）

例如：

It's nice helping you.

幫助你感覺真不錯。（已經幫助了）

It's nice to do the job.

做這份工作會很不錯的。（即將開始做）

# Unit 5 朋友多,路好走 Making Friends

## Fresh Expressions

A friend in need is a friend indeed.

患難見真情。

A true friend is forever a friend.

真正的朋友是一輩子的朋友。

A man should keep his friendship in constant repair.

只有經常「澆灌」,方能保持友誼天長地久。

All the splendor in the world is not worth a good friend.

人世間所有的榮華富貴不如一個好朋友。

Don't try to win a friend by presenting gifts. You should instead contribute your sincere love and learn how to win others' heart through appropriate ways.

不要靠饋贈去獲得朋友。你必須奉獻你誠摯的愛,學會怎麼用正當的方法來贏得別人的心。

Friendship is an essential ingredient in the making of a healthful, rewarding life.

友誼是使人的一生健康而有意義所不可缺少的組成部分。

## Interactive Dialogues

### Dialogue 1

A:What's the matter, Susan? You look very tense. Anything wrong?

A:怎麼了,蘇珊?妳看起來很緊張。出什麼事了嗎?

B:It' my mother. She is in the hospital. I just got a call from the hospital.

B:是我媽媽。她住院了。我剛從醫院那裡接到電話。

33

A：What about her?

A：她怎麼了？

B：She has had heart problems for quite some time and the doctor said that she needs a bypass right away.

B：她的心臟問題已有好長一段時間了，醫生說她需要馬上做繞道手術。

A：I'm sorry to hear that. Why don't you take some days off and stay with your mom in the hospital? She needs you there.

A：聽到這個消息我很難過。妳為什麼不請假，在醫院陪妳媽呢？她那裡需要你。

B：I know. But what she needs most is money for the heart surgery right now. I had asked all my relatives and all the people I could think of. I am still short of some money.

B：我知道。但是她現在最需要的是馬上進行心臟手術的錢。我已請求我的所有親戚和我能想到的人，但是我還是沒湊齊錢。

A：How much more do you need? See if I could help you.

A：妳還需要多少錢呢？看看我是否能幫妳。

B：Three thousand.

B：三千。

A：I have two thousands in my savings and I will call my boy friend for the balance.

A：我有兩千塊的儲蓄，剩下的我來打電話給我男朋友。

B：Joe, it is so kind of you. I don't know how to thank you enough.

B：喬，妳真好。我不知道怎麼感謝妳。

A：Susan, please don't mention it. That is what friends are for. A friend in need is a friend indeed. Let me call my boy friend right now.

A：蘇珊，別客氣。這是朋友應該做的。患難見真情。我馬上就打電話給我男朋友。

B：Let me write it down the amount I borrow from you. As soon as I get the money, I will return it back to you.

B：我來寫下妳借我錢的總數，只要我拿到錢，我就立刻還妳。

A：Don't worry about it. OK. My boy friend said we could go and get the money now. Let's go.

A：別擔心。好。我男朋友說我們現在能過去拿錢了。走吧！

B：Great, Joe, a million thanks.

B：太好了，喬，萬分感謝。

### Notes

- tense（心理或神經）緊張的；引起緊張的。例如：
  The situation suddenly became tense.
  局勢突然變得緊張起來。
- balance 有「平衡」的基本涵義，但也有「剩餘部分」的意思，the balance 指的就是「差額、其餘」。
- don't mention it 用在你幫助別人後，別人向你致謝時說的話；而 no problem 就是指別人需要你的幫助，你答應別人。
- a million thanks 也常說成 thanks a million，是一種誇張的說法，表示「萬分感謝」的意思。

Dialogue 2

A：So how long have you known Mark?

A：所以你認識馬克有多久了？

B：We go way back. We've known each other since we were toddlers.

B：我們早就認識了。從學走路時就在一起了。

A：Really? You guys must be really tight.

A：真的嗎？一定很親密。

B：Yeah, We're buddy-buddy still.

B：對，我們就像親兄弟不分彼此。

A：He seems sincere, and trustworthy.

A：他看起來很真誠，值得信任。

B：Well, he is, but he can be conniving at times.

B：嗯，他是這樣。不過有時也滿滑頭的。

A：What do you mean?

A：什麼意思？

B：Well, I know that he would never stab me in the back. But I've seen him double-cross other people.

B：嗯，我知道他絕不會誹謗我。不過我知道他曾搬弄別人的是非。

A：Oh, my! Really? I never thought he would be like that.

A：哦，天哪！真的嗎？真沒想到他是這種人。

B：Don't get me wrong, I'm not saying he's like that all the time.

B：可別曲解我的意思，我並不是說他一直都是那樣。

A：So, can I trust him or what?

A：那，我能夠信任他嗎？

B：Well, I think you should decide for yourself.

B：嗯，我想你應該自己決定。

A：But I need someone that I can count on for this job.

A：但我需要一些我可以信任的人來做這份工作。

B：Okay, Okay. You can trust him. I was just trying to give you a hard time.

B：好的，好。你可以信任他。我只是想刁難刁難你。

A：Come on you're confusing me. Give it to me straight.

A：你把我弄糊塗了。直接告訴我。

B：Actually, he's the most dependable person I know, and he would never turn on anyone.

B：其實，他是我知道的人中最值得信賴的人，他不會出賣任何人。

## Notes

- go way back 這是一個口語表達，意思是「有交情；兩個人在一起很長時間」。在美劇中常常會用到。
- toddler 意為「學步的小孩；蹣跚行走者」。例如：
  The toddler tried to walk but kept falling down.
  那小孩學著走路但老是跌倒。
- tight 這個詞除了形容某物很嚴密、很緊、很牢固之外，還可用來形容人的關係很親密。
- buddy-buddy 是一個俚語說法，意為「很親密的、非常親密的」。例如：
  I am buddy-buddy with him.
  我和他是非常要好的朋友。

但單獨一個 buddy 是名詞，表示好朋友。例如：

He is my buddy.

他是我的好朋友。

■ trustworthy 是由 trust+worthy 組成的，意為「值得信賴的；可信的；可靠的」。例如：

He is an experienced and trustworthy guide.

他是一位有經驗的、可信賴的嚮導。

■ at times 意為「有時、間或」。例如：

Everyone may make mistakes at times.

每個人不時都會犯錯。

■ stab sb. in the back 字面意思是指在某人背後插一刀，引申為背叛（某人）或辜負其信任。其實就是「放冷箭」。例如：

Such a vicious lie is nothing but a stab in the back.

這種惡毒的謊言完全是暗箭傷人。

■ double-cross 是口語說法，意為「背叛；詐欺；出賣」。double-cross 也可寫成 doubleX。例如：

After he double-crossed his best friend, everyone gave him the cold shoulder.

在他出賣了最好的朋友後，每個人對他十分冷淡。

■ count on sb. 意為「依賴；依靠；期待；指望」。例如：

Can I count on your help? = Can I count on you to help me?

我能指望你的幫助嗎？

■ give sb. a hard time 意為「使某人難堪；和某人過不去；給……帶來困難、難題」。

■ give it to sb. straight 意為「坦白的告訴某人」。

# Chapter2
# 出行求助 Nice Trip

## Unit 1 向別人問路 Asking the Way

### Fresh Expressions

Excuse me, can you tell me how can I get to the Wangfujing Street?

打擾一下，請問王府井大街該怎麼去？

Could you tell me the way to the Pacific Hotel?

請問去太平洋飯店該怎麼走？

How can I get to the railway station?

到火車站該怎麼走？

How can I get to the subway station?

請問我怎麼去地鐵站？

Excuse me. How can I get to the nearest post office?

請問去最近的郵局怎麼走？

Excuse me, Where am I on this map?

對不起，請問我在地圖上的什麼地方？

About how long will it take me to get there?

去那裡大約要花多少時間？

Sorry to trouble you, but could you direct me to the bus station?

對不起打擾您，請問您能幫我指一下到公車站的路嗎？

Is this the right way to the nearest department store?

去附近的百貨公司是不是走這條路？

## Interactive Dialogues

### Dialogue 1

A：Excuse me. Sorry to trouble you, but is this the right way to the nearest department store?

A：不好意思。打擾一下，去附近的百貨公司是不是走這條路呢？

B：I'm afraid you're going in the opposite direction.

B：恐怕你走了相反的方向。

A：I'm sorry to hear that. But could you tell me how to get there? I'm new here, you know.

A：太遺憾了。但你能告訴我該怎麼走嗎？你知道，我剛來這裡不久。

B：OK. I'll show you the way. Turn back and go straight down the street to the traffic lights. Then turn to the left and you'll be in the Rose Street. Keep on walking along the street for about 200 meters and take the first turn on your right. The department store is there near the corner. You can't miss it.

B：好。我來指給你看。向後轉，沿著這條街一直走到紅綠燈處。然後向左轉，這時你就在玫瑰街了。順著這條街再繼續走 200 公尺左右，到第一條馬路往右轉。百貨公司就在角落附近。你不會錯過它的。

A：About how long will it take me to get there? Is it far to walk?

A：去那裡大約要花多久時間？ 走去會很遠嗎？

B：No, it's no distance at all. You can walk it within ten minutes.

B：不，一點也不遠。只要 10 分鐘就能走到了。

A：Thank you very much for your help.

A：多謝你的幫助。

B：You're welcome.

B：不用客氣。

Notes

■ go straight down... 這裡的 straight 是副詞，表示「直接地、一直地」。
例如：

I'll come straight home after work.

下班後我直接回家。

■ 在 down the street 這個詞組中，down 用作介詞，和 along（沿著）的
意思差不多。

Keep on walking... 在這句中：keep on 相當於 continue，表示繼續的意
思，後接動名詞詞組。

■ take the first turn on your right 的意思是：到第一條馬路向右轉。如果
說「第二個路口向左轉」，你可以這樣用英文表達：take the second
turn on your left。

■ You can't miss it. 這句話直譯的意思是「你不會沒看見的」。此處的
miss 意為「錯過、沒看到」。它還可以表示「沒聽到、沒察覺到」。
例如：

I missed the first part of the speech.

我沒聽到演講的第一部分。

Dialogue 2

A：Excuse me. Could you tell me how to get to the Palace Museum?

A：對不起。請問到皇家博物館怎麼走？

B：You can take a No. 1 bus. The conductor will tell you where to get off.

B：你可以搭 1 號公車，售票員會告訴你在哪裡下車。

A：Yes, but I'm driving my own car.

A：是的，但我要自己開車去。

B：Oh, then you drive along this street, turn left at the second crossroad, then take the first right. Keep straight on until you see a road sign that says "Palace Hotel," and then you follow the sign. It will direct you to the Palace Museum.

B：哦，那你沿著這條街開，在第二個十字路口左轉，然後在第一個轉彎處右轉。一直走，然後你會看到一個寫著「皇家酒店」的路標，跟著它的指示走就對了。它會帶你到皇家博物館的。

A：Drive along this street, turn left, turn right, keep straight, and then I'll see the road sign?

A：沿著這條街開，左轉，右轉，直走，然後就會看到路標？

B：That's right. Well...I don't see any car around here. Where is your car?

B：沒錯。嗯……我沒看到這附近有車。你的車停在哪裡？

A：I parked it over there. You see?

A：就在那邊。妳看到了嗎？

B：Oh, no. You'd better move it before a policeman sees you parking there.

B：哦，糟糕。你最好趁警察還沒來以前趕緊開走。

A：Why? I don't see any "No Parking" signs.

A：為什麼？我沒看到有「禁止停車」的標誌。

B：But you're parking in a bus zone.

B：但是你停在公車區。

A：Here comes a policeman. I'd better run. Thank you, miss. Oh, by the way, how long will it take for me to get to the museum?

A：警察來了。我最好趕快走。謝謝妳了，小姐。哦，對了，到皇家博物館大概要花多少時間？

B：About half an hour.

B：大約半小時。

A：Thanks again. You've been very helpful.

A：再次謝謝妳。妳幫了大忙。

B：Hurry up, or you'll get a ticket.

B：快點，否則你就會收到罰單了。

**Notes**

- direct sb. to 意為「給某人指路」。direct 是「指引」的意思。當它後面接一個地點時翻譯為指路，也就是指引某人去某地。如果接 do sth.，代表指引某人去做一件事，在語境中翻譯過來為「命令某人做某事」。

- Here comes a policeman. 這句話是由 here 開頭的完全倒裝句。在「副詞 here、there、now、then 等 + be、go、come 等動詞的一般現在式 + 名詞充當的主語」句型中，總是用完全倒裝。這時，一般現在式常可表達進行概念。這句話的一般語序為：A policeman comes here. 注意：但主語若是人稱代詞時，謂語部分不倒裝。例如：Here he comes.（主語是第三人稱代詞 he）

# Unit 2 如何乘車 How to Take a Bus or Subway

## Fresh Expressions

Excuse me, does the bus go to the airport？

不好意思，請問這輛公車去機場嗎？

Excuse me, can you tell me which bus goes to the airport?

不好意思，請問幾號公車去機場？

Can you tell me where to change?

請問在哪裡轉車呢？

Where should I get off?

我該在哪裡下車呢？

Walk a block and turn left, then you'll find a bus stop.

過一個街區左轉，你就到公車站了。

Take the No. 11 bus, which goes to the airport.

搭 11 號公車，它去機場。

You'll have to change buses.

你需要轉車。

You can get off at the Queen Cinema and then change to a No. 28 bus.

你可以在皇后戲院下車，然後再轉搭 28 號公車。

You've got on the wrong bus. You should take a No. 10 bus.

你坐錯車了。你該搭 10 號公車。

Take the same number bus in the opposite direction, and change to No. 12 bus.

搭反方向的同一號碼公車，然後再轉搭 12 號公車。

The first subway pulls in there at 5:00 a.m.

首班列車在早上 5 點進站。

Do I have to pay an additional fare to change subways?

轉乘地鐵還要付費嗎？

Go to the Xizhimen Station to Switch to Railway No. 13.

到西直門換搭 13 號線地鐵。

You can get almost anywhere rather quickly on a subway.

你可以坐地鐵迅速到達任何地方。

## Interactive Dialogues

Dialogue 1

A：Does this bus go down to the Central Square?

A：這輛公車去中央廣場嗎？

B：I'm sorry. This bus doesn't go that far. It only goes as far as the Rose Park.

B：對不起。這輛車沒去那麼遠。它只到玫瑰公園。

A：But I was told to take this bus there. Isn't it a No. 48 bus?

A：但有人告訴我坐這輛公車。這不是 48 號公車嗎？

B：No, it's a No. 84. You've got on the wrong bus. Let me tell you what you can do. Our two lines have the same stop at the Grand Theatre. You can get off there, then change to a No. 48 bus at the same stop.

B：不，這是 84 號。你搭錯車了。我告訴你該怎麼辦。我們這兩線路公車在大劇院是同一站。你可以在那裡下車，然後再轉搭 48 號公車。

A：OK. But is the Rose Park far from the Central Square?

A：好的。但玫瑰公園離中央廣場還很遠嗎？

B：Not very far. It's one stop further. You can walk it within ten minutes.

B：不太遠。再往前走一站，10 分鐘就能到。

A：Then I might as well take this bus to the terminal and walk the rest of the way.

A：那我還是搭這輛公車到終點站，剩下的路我走過去。

B：All right. Then pass down the bus, please.

B：可以。那麼請往裡面走。

A：Thank you.

A：謝謝。

**Notes**

■ that far 這裡的 that 用作普通副詞，相當於 so 的意思。這種用法在口語中常常會碰到。例如：

Is the problem that easy?

問題有那麼簡單嗎？

■ get on 意為「上車」，get off 意為「下車」。

■ might as well 的意思是「不妨」、「倒不如」、「還是……的好」，屬於固定搭配。類似表達還有：may as well、could as well 也表示同樣的意思。例如：

We may/might just as well have a try.

試一下未嘗不可。

■ within ten minutes10 分鐘之內。

■ the rest of the way 剩下的路。

Dialogue 2

A：Let's go to Wangfujing by bus.

A：我們坐公車去王府井吧！

B：Better take the subway. It's faster, and more convenient.

B：最好搭地鐵。地鐵更快，更方便。

A：OK, it will be a new experience for me.

A：好，這對我來說將是個新的經驗。

B：We have a rather comprehensive subway system here. You can get almost anywhere rather quickly on a subway, especially at this time of day when the traffic is heavy....

B：我們這裡有相當廣泛的地鐵系統。你可以搭地鐵迅速到達任何地方，尤其是在交通高峰期……。

A：Where do we pay the fare?

A：我們在哪裡付車資？

B：Just give the man standing there 2 yuan and he'll give you a token. Then, you slip it into the slot at the turnstile and push the turnstile to get in.

B：只要給售票人員 2 元，他會給你一個代幣。你在入口處那裡把代幣塞進投幣孔，就能推轉門進去了。

A：Let me pay for it. Where can I get a subway map?

A：讓我來付費。我在哪裡能拿到地鐵地圖？

B：Ask the worker who sells tokens to give you one. It's free of charge. Actually maps showing subway routes are posted at most stations.

B：向售票人員要一張。那是免費的。實際上大多數地鐵站都貼有線路圖。

A：Do I have to pay an additional fare to change trains?

A：轉搭地鐵時，我還要付費嗎？

B：No, you don't have to. Here comes the train.

B：不用。車來了。

A：Be careful! Subway doors open and close automatically.

A：小心！車門是自動開關的。

B：Well, it's not as crowded as we expected, isn't it?

B：嗯，沒有我們想像的那麼擁擠，對吧？

A：No, but it will be soon. Look, there're two empty seats over there. Let's get them.

A：是，但很快就會擁擠。看，那邊有兩個空位，我們去坐吧！

B：Now let's make ourselves comfortable since we've got quite a long way to go.

B：走了這麼多路，讓我們舒服一下。

Notes

■ Better take the subway. 在這句話中，better 是 You'd better 的簡化口語形式，所以後面用動詞原形 take。

■ rather 的用法如下：

・rather 可修飾像 ugly、dirty 之類的貶義形容詞、副詞。例如：
His hands are rather dirty.
He is a rather ugly man.

・rather 也可以修飾褒獎的形容詞、副詞，其含義相當於 very。例如：
This picture is rather fine, isn't it?
He runs rather fast.

・rather 還可修飾動詞或過去分詞，其意思是「有點」。例如：
We rather like the smell.
I felt rather tired.

・rather 與 too 連用時，表示「稍微……一點」，修飾形容詞或副詞。例如：
The book is rather too difficult.

・rather 修飾名詞前的形容詞時，放在不定冠詞前後均可；若無形容詞，rather 應放在不定冠詞前面。例如：
It's a rather hot day. = It's rather a hot day.
The girl is rather a fool.

■ slip into 使滑入；塞進。例如：
All you have to do is break concentration once and you will slip into a

dream pool.

- turnstile 懸轉門；旋轉式柵門。push the turnstile 推動轉門

- free of charge 不收費；免費。例如：

We will deliver it free of charge.

我們免費送貨。

# Unit 3 火車站諮詢 Train Station

## Fresh Expressions

Where is the ticket office?

售票處在哪裡？

Tickets to Paris have been sold out.

到巴黎的票賣完了。

Sleepers are not available now.

沒有臥鋪了。

I'm afraid only one-way tickets are available.

恐怕只有單程票了。

Wait a moment, please. I'll check the berth chart.

請稍等。我查一下臥鋪登記表。

Would you like an upper berth or a lower berth?

你喜歡上鋪還是下鋪？

Where should I board the train for Taipei?

請問去臺北的火車在哪裡搭？

It gets here at 7:00, stays for fifteen minutes and it reaches the destination at 1 o'clock in the afternoon.

這輛車 7：00 到這裡，停 15 分鐘，到達目的地是下午 1 點整。

I want to reserve a seat on the international train to Paris.

我要預訂一張去巴黎的國際列車車票。

I want to a window seat so that I can enjoy the pretty sights during the journey.

我想要靠窗的座位，以便欣賞沿途的美景。

The booking office usually sells tickets three days in advance.

售票處通常都提前 3 天售票。

All non-passengers leave the train right away, please.

請送親友的馬上下車。

Please have your tickets ready for conductor.

請您將車票準備好讓驗票員檢驗。

## Interactive Dialogues

### Dialogue 1

A：May I help you, sir?

A：我可以幫您什麼忙嗎？

B：Yes, I'd like some information about the trains to Taipei.

B：我想知道一些去臺北的火車資訊。

A：When do you want to go?

A：您想什麼時候去？

B：On July 7, I have to be there well before twelve o'clock.

B：7 月 7 日。我得在 12 點之前趕到那裡。

A：There's a train at 7 a.m. It'll get you there at 11 a.m. But there are many stops along the way.

A：有一輛上午 7 點的車，上午 11 點到達。但在路上會停好幾站。

B：And I have to get up early, too. Are there any nonstops to Taipei?

B：我還得早起，有沒有直達臺北的車？

A：Yes, there is one at 8:30 a.m. That arrives at 11:35 a.m.

A：有一輛上午 8 點 30 分的車，在上午 11 點 35 分到達。

B：I think the 8:30 will be better. What's the fare?

B：我想 8 點半這輛車更合適。票價是多少？

A：Do you want to buy a single or round trip ticket?

A：您要單程票還是來回票？

B：What's the difference between them?

B：有什麼不同嗎？

A：A round trip ticket saves you about 10 percent of the fare. Do you prefer a first class ticket or a second class?

A：來回票為您節省 10%的票價，您要頭等票還是二等票呢？

B：A second class. So how much is it?

B：二等票。多少錢呢？

A：Fifty dollars.

A：50 美元。

B：Can I buy my ticket here?

B：我可以在這裡買票嗎？

A：No, sir. We deal only with enquiries. You have to get your ticket at the booking office outside this door on the left.

A：不能，先生。我們只回答詢問。您應該在門外左邊的購票處買票。

B：Thanks for the information.

B：謝謝你提供的訊息。

A：Please don't stand on ceremony. It's just my duty.

A：別客氣，這是我的職責。

**Notes**

first class、second class、third class

travel first class（坐頭等廂／艙），可指火車、飛機、輪船等的頭等廂
／艙。就火車而言，first class 指軟臥、硬臥是 second class、硬坐是 third
class。這個分法貌似是給老外看的，對國人來說，軟臥、硬臥大家都清
楚，不過你介紹給老外時就可以派上用場了。

2. stand on 有「強調」、「堅持」或「拘泥於」等意思。ceremony 意
為「禮儀、禮節」，故詞組 stand on ceremony 就是意指「講究禮儀、默守
禮法」或「拘泥於禮節」，與「客氣」近似。如：

Please don't stand on ceremony.

請不要客氣。

Dialogue 2

A：Hello. Good morning.

A：哈囉，早安。

B：Hello. Ticket Office. Can I help you?

B：您好。這裡是售票處。我能為您做些什麼？

A：I would like to buy a ticket for special express to Beijing.

A：我想買一張往北京的特快列車車票。

B：Sure. The booking office usually sells tickets three days in advance.
Would you please tell me which train you want to take and what date you plan to
leave?

B：當然可以。售票處通常提前 3 天售票。請告訴我您想乘坐哪輛車，哪天出發？

A：Well, I plan to depart on 28th this month. But I don't know which train it is the best for me to take. Can you recommend it for me?

A：嗯，我打算這個月 28 日出發。但是我不知道坐哪輛車最合適。你能推薦給我嗎？

B：All right. Let me see.... Oh, you can take the special train T12 to Beijing at 5:30 p.m. on April 28th.

B：好的。讓我看看……。哦，你可以搭乘 4 月 28 日下午 5 點 30 分前往北京的 T12 特快列車。

A：OK. I'll take it. Thank you. How much does it cost?

A：好的。我就坐這輛。謝謝你。多少錢？

B：256RMB.

B：256 元人民幣。

A：Oh. By the way, can you give me the seat by the windows?

A：哦。對了，你能給我靠窗的座位嗎？

B：Of course. Here you are.

B：當然可以。您的票在這。

A：Thank you so much. Bye!

A：非常感謝，再見！

B：Bye! Wish you a good trip!

B：再見！祝您旅途愉快！

**Notes**

- I'll take it. = I'll buy it. 就是我要買它的意思，但是比後者更加婉轉，更加客氣。不可以理解為我要拿走它。

# Unit 4 機場協助一瞥 Airport Situation

## Fresh Expressions

I'd like to book a ticket to Shanghai.

我想訂一張去上海的機票。

I want to fly to Taipei on or about the first.

我想買下個月 1 號左右去臺北的機票。

Do you have a flight to Tokyo departing at about 10 am Next Monday?

你們有下週一大約下午 10 點起飛到東京的班機嗎？

Please call the Airlines Booking Office three days before your departure date for reconfirmation.

請在飛機起飛 3 天前打電話到航空售票處再次確認。

Now I'm taking a flight on Friday instead.

我現在要改搭星期五的班機。

Please help me cancel the ticket for flight BE 344, and book one seat on flight BE 346 to Paris.

請幫我取消英航 344 班機的機票，改訂英航 346 號飛往巴黎的班機。

Would you like a single or a return ticket?

您要買單程還是來回票？

I am sorry. The flight is fully booked for the 20th.

很抱歉，20 日的機票全賣完了。

You'd better reach the airport one hour before departure time for check in.

您最好在機場驗票前一小時到達機場。

Would you show me the fastest way to get there?

可以請你告訴我到那裡最快的方法嗎？

They're calling your flight now. You barely have time to make it.

現在正在報你的班機起飛時間呢。你勉強能夠趕上。

We are now boarding all passengers on flight 123 to Sydney.

乘坐飛往雪梨的 123 次航班的旅客現在請登機。

## Interactive Dialogues

### Dialogue 1

A：To which gate do I need to go to catch connecting flight 101 to New York City?

A：我要在哪個登機門轉乘 101 班機前往紐約？

B：Go to gate 18. The plane is now boarding. You must hurry.

B：到 18 號門。這趟班機已經在登機了。你要趕快。

A：Show me the fastest way to get there.

A：告訴我到那裡最快的方法。

B：Instead of walking, you can take this shuttle to get you there faster.

B：別走路，你搭機場的穿梭車，就可以比較快到達那裡。

A：Do you think the plane will leave without me?

A：你想飛機會不會不等我就起飛呢？

B：No, I'll call the attendants at the gate. I will tell them you're on your way.

B：不會，我會打電話給機場門的服務人員。我會告訴他們你已經在途中了。

A：Thank you so much. I would really appreciate that.

A：多謝。我真的很感激你的協助。

B：You are welcome. Have a safe trip.

B：不用客氣，祝你旅途平安。

### Notes

- connecting flight 就是表示「中轉班機」的意思。如果你乘坐的飛機不是直達目的地的話，那麼你在轉接班機機場，就要用 connecting flight 來詢問地乘人員。

- flight attendant 是「空中服務員、空姐、空服人員」的意思，有時也稱 steward（男空服員）或 stewardess（女空服員）。例如：

Is Mary a flight attendant?

瑪莉是空服員嗎？

### Dialogue 2

A：Good morning, Carol.

A：卡羅，早安。

B：Good morning, sir. What can I do for you?

B：先生，您早。有什麼我可以效勞的嗎？

A：Yes. It says on my tickets...I am supposed to change to flight NH-803 at Bangkok, for Stockholm.

A：是的。我的機票上寫著……我應該在曼谷轉搭 NH-803 的班機去斯德哥爾摩。

B：Yes, sir. But can I see your tickets first, just to make sure.

B：好的，先生。我可以看看您的機票嗎？只是確認一下。

A：Certainly, here is my ticket.

A：當然，機票在這裡。

B：You are right, sir. You are supposed to change to your connecting flight NH-803 for Stockholm at Bangkok.

B：沒錯，先生。您應該在曼谷轉搭 NH-803 班機到斯德哥爾摩。

A：Do you think I have enough time for my connecting flight?

A：你覺得我轉機的時間夠嗎？

B：I think so. And we will let you have the top priority to get off the aircraft when arriving at Bangkok.

B：應該夠。到達曼谷時，我們會讓您優先下機。

A：That's very nice of you to do so.

A：這樣非常好。

B：You are welcome. But we do this to all transfer passengers.

B：不客氣。我們都會讓要轉機的旅客優先下機。

### Notes

- It says on... 意為「在……上寫道，在……上說」。例如：

  It says on the packet that these crisps contain no additives.

  包裝上說這些炸薯片不含添加劑。

- be supposed to do 主語是「人」時，意為「應該、被期望做……」。它可以用來表示勸告、建議、義務、責任等，相當於情態動詞 should。例如：

You are supposed to shake hands when you meet someone for the first time in Taiwan.

在臺灣你與他人第一次見面時，應該握手。

當 be supposed to... 的主語是「物」時，它表示「本應；本該」，用於表示「某事本應該發生而沒有發生」。例如：

The train was supposed to arrive half an hour ago.

火車本應在半小時之前到達。

be supposed to 後面接「have + 過去分詞」時，表示「本應該做某事而沒做」。例如：

He is supposed to have arrived an hour ago.

他應該一小時前就到了。

be supposed to... 的否定結構為 be not supposed to...，它常用於口語中，意為「不被許可；不應當」。例如：

You are not supposed to smoke on the bus.

你不應該在公車上吸菸。

■ top priority 意為「優先考慮；最先處理」。例如：

Security is a top priority.

安全是應予最優先考慮的事。

# Chapter3
## 日常瑣事 Daily Matters

## Unit 1 求租房屋 House Hunting

### Fresh Expressions

When do you think is convenient to see the room?

你什麼時候方便去看房間？

Can you tell me your present address?

你能告訴我你現在的地址嗎？

Usually a house is too expensive for the salary-earning class to buy.

通常房子太貴，領薪族買不起。

Most unfurnished apartments have heating systems, air conditioners, and refrigerators.

沒有家具的公寓大部分都有供暖系統、空調和冰箱。

We expect a vacancy in two weeks.

我們期望兩週之內有空房。

Are the utilities included in the rent?

水電費也算在房租裡嗎？

Could you estimate how much a single person would have to pay for utilities each month?

您估計一個人每月要付多少水電費？

You can't sublet the apartment.

你不能把這間公寓轉租給他人。

The building may be a little old, but the structure is very sturdy.

房子可能舊了點，但結構很穩固。

What's the rent for an efficiency apartment?

一間經濟型公寓的房租是多少？

Can I buy on installments?

我可以分期付款嗎？

I like the house very much because it faces the south.

我喜歡這房子因為它朝南。

We are on the 18th floor, so there's a very nice view from the balcony.

我們住在 18 層，從陽臺看出去風景很美。

## Interactive Dialogues

### Dialogue 1

A：Hello. I hear you have an apartment for rent.

A：你好，聽說你有房要出租。

B：Yep. We have one coming up the first of June.

B：是的。有一間到 6 月 1 號可以出租。

A：Is it a two-bedroom?

A：是兩室一廳的嗎？

B：Two bedrooms, a nice living-dining area, a complete kitchen, and a full bathroom.

B：有 2 個臥室，一個很好的餐廳，一個完整的廚房和一個可以洗澡的洗手間。

A：How much is it?

A：多少錢呢？

B：Eight hundred per month with one month refundable deposit.

B：每月 800 元，外加一個月可退還的押金。

A：Do I have to sign a lease?

A：我是否需要簽租約？

B：Yes, it's a one-year lease.

B：是的，要簽一份一年的租約。

A：Well, perhaps I should have a look at the apartment first.

A：嗯，也許我該先看看房子。

B：Sure. Wait a moment and I'll get the key. Here's the living room. You see there are big closets.

B：當然。等一下，我拿鑰匙。這是客廳，你看有很大的衣櫥。

A：Are the utilities included in the rent?

A：水電費也算在房租內嗎？

B：We split the gas, electricity and water. You may have your own tele-phone and phone bill.

B：我們平分瓦斯費、電費和水費。你可以自己裝電話，自己承擔費用。

A：Is there a washer?

A：有洗衣機嗎？

B：Yes. You can use them anytime between 8 a.m. and 10 p.m., but we close it after that. People might sleep or study, you know. What do you think of the apartment?

B：有。你可以在早上 8 點到晚上 10 點之間使用，但超過時間不能用。你知道，有人可能在睡覺或讀書。你覺得房子怎麼樣？

A：This furnished apartment with a kitchen really fits me, although it does need a fresh coat of paint. It's a good place. I'll have to think about it. Can I call you next Monday?

A：帶家具和廚房的房子蠻適合我的，儘管牆上還需要粉刷一下。這個地方不錯。我還要考慮考慮。下週一回電給你好嗎？

B：Sure, if you want. But someone else may take it. This is a busy time.

B：當然可以。但也許別人會要，這段時間租房的人很多。

### Notes

- for rent 意為「出租」。
- have a look at 也是「看」的意思，但表示看什麼具體的東西，而且 at 後面要接受詞。have a look 是一個詞組，意思是「看一看」，後面不接受詞。
- utilities 指的是水電、煤氣、暖氣等雜費。
- a fresh coat of paint 刷一層油漆。這裡 coat 不能解釋為「大衣」，而要譯為「塗層」。paint 當名詞，是「油漆、塗料」的意思。

### Dialogue 2

A：I saw your advertisement in this morning's New York Times, and I'd like to take a look at the apartment.

A：我在今天早上的紐約時報看到你們的廣告，所以我來看一下公寓。

B：Come in, please. It's on the second floor. This way, please.

B：請進。公寓在二樓。這邊請。

A：How much does the apartment rent for?

A：請問這間公寓租金怎麼算？

B：It's three hundred dollars a month. Here we are. This is the living room. There are windows in every room. The kitchen is on your left.

B：一個月三百塊。我們到了。這是客廳。每個房間都有窗戶。廚房在你的左邊。

A：There are two bathrooms. That's great!

A：有兩間浴室。太棒了！

B：By the way, we don't allow any pets here.

B：對了，我們這裡不准養寵物。

A：I see. What about decorating?

A：我知道了。那裝潢呢？

B：If you decide to move in, we will repaint the apartment on the condition that you sign a two-year lease.

B：如果你決定要入住，我們會幫你重新油漆整間公寓，條件是你簽2 年的租約。

A：That means if I sign a one-year lease, there will be no redecorating at all?

A：那就是說，如果我只簽 1 年租約，就不會重新裝潢了？

B：That's right.

B：沒錯。

A：If I decided to take it, how soon could I move in?

A：如果我決定要租這間公寓，最快什麼時候可以搬進來？

B：You can move in any time you like. As you can see, it's already cleaned up.

B：你隨時可以搬進來。如你所見，公寓已經打掃乾淨了。

A：Good. Er...Mrs....?

A：很好。呃，妳是……？

B：Jones.

B：瓊斯。

A：Mrs. Jones, I like this apartment very much, but I'd like to know my wife's and kids' opinions. I'll come back this evening with them. Will that be convenient?

A：瓊斯太太，我很喜歡這間公寓，不過我想聽聽我太太和孩子們的看法。我晚上再和他們一起來，不知道方不方便？

B：That's fine with me.

B：我沒問題。

A：This is my business card. Thanks very much, Mrs. Jones. We'll see you tonight.

A：這是我的名片。謝謝妳，瓊斯太太。晚上見。

## Notes

- 在美式英文中，樓房地面與街道相平的樓層叫 first floor，first floor 上面一層叫 second floor，也就是「二樓」。

  在英式英文中，樓房地面與街道相平的樓層叫 ground floor，ground floor 上面一層叫 first floor，也就是「二樓」。

  move in 意為「住進、搬入（住宅）」；「使（某人）搬進」。例如：

  We have just moved in.

  我們才剛搬進來。

- on the condition that 的意思是「如果；假如」。例如：

I will go on condition that you will too.

如果你也去，我才會去。

- clean up 意為「打掃；整理」。例如：

She is cleaning up the kitchen now.

她現在正在打掃廚房。

# Unit 2 求醫問藥 Seeing a Doctor

## Fresh Expressions

I feel a bit off color.

我感到有點不適。

I feel a pain in my abdomen.

我覺得肚子痛。

I feel dizzy and I've got no appetite.

我覺得頭暈，沒有食慾。

I have a spitting headache.

我頭痛得厲害。

The toothache is simply unbearable.

牙痛讓人受不了。

My nose is stuffed up. I have a sore throat.

我有點鼻塞。喉嚨很痛。

I feel a pulsating pain at my temple.

我的太陽穴好像在激烈震動一樣地痛。

Here's a prescription for some medicine.

這是藥方。

I'll give you some tablets.

我給你開些藥片。

These pills are for your fever and indigestion.

這些藥丸是治療您的發燒和消化不良的。

I'll give you some cough medicine and some antibiotic pills.

我給您開點咳嗽藥和一些抗生素藥片。

Take these medicines after meals twice a day.

這些藥一天服兩次，飯後服用。

## Interactive Dialogue

### Dialogue 1

A：Good morning.

A：早安。

B：Good morning.

B：早安。

A：What seems to be the problem ？

A：請問哪裡不舒服？

B：I'm running a high fever and feeling terribly bad.

B：我發高燒，感覺糟透了。

A：How long have you had the problem ？

A：這種情況出現多久了？

B：Since last night.

B：從昨晚開始的。

A：OK. In that case, you have to fill in this registration card. Your age, gender, address and things like that.

A：好的，那麼您得先填寫這張掛號表。比如您的年齡、性別、住址等等。

B：No problem. Which department should I register with, madam？

B：沒問題。請問我應該掛哪科呢，女士？

A：You'd better go to the medical department.

A：您最好掛內科。

B：(Two minutes later) Here is my registration card.

B：（兩分鐘後）表填好了。

A：Thank you. The registration fee is one dollar.

A：謝謝。掛號費是 1 美元。

B：Fine. But can you tell me how to get to the medical department, please？

B：好的。請問我該怎麼走？

A：Take the lift to the third floor and then make a left turn. Go along the corridor until you see the sign on your right.

A：坐電梯到三樓，左轉。沿著走道直到您看到右手邊的標示。

B：Thanks a lot.

B：多謝了。

A：You're welcome.

A：不客氣。

| Notes |

■ 表達「你哪裡不舒服」的說法有：

What seems to be the problem?

What's the matter with you?

What's wrong with you?

What's the problem?

What's going on?

What happened?

- run a high fever 發高燒，注意要用「run」這個單字。還可以改成 run a temperature。

- had better（常簡略為 'd better）是一固定詞組，had better 表示「最好」的意思，用於表示對別人的勸告、建議或表示一種願望。had better 後跟動詞原形（即不帶 to 的不定式），構成 had better do sth. 句型。這裡的 had 不能用 have 來替換。例如：

You'd better go to hospital at once.

你最好立即去醫院看病。

此外，had better 的否定式常用的形式是將否定副詞 not 直接放在 had better 後面。否定副詞 not 絕不能放在 had 後面。例如：

You had better not miss the last bus.

你最好不要錯過末班公車。

## Dialogue 2

A：Good morning. What's the matter with you?

A：早安。你哪裡不舒服？

B：Good morning, doctor. I have a terrible headache.

B：早安，醫生。我頭痛得厲害。

A：All right, young man. Tell me how it got started.

A：好的，年輕人。告訴我怎麼回事。

B：Yesterday I had a running nose. Now my nose is stuffed-up. I have a sore throat. And I'm afraid I've got a temperature. I feel terrible.

B：昨天我流鼻涕。現在有點鼻塞。喉嚨很痛。恐怕還有發燒。感覺糟透了。

A：Don't worry, young man. Let me give you an examination. First let me take a look at your throat. Open your mouth and say "ah...."

A：別擔心，年輕人。讓我幫你檢查一下。我先看看你的喉嚨。張開嘴說「啊」。

B：Ah.

B：啊。

A：Good. Now put your tongue out. All right, let me examine your chest. Please unbutton your shirt. Let me check your heart and lungs. Take a deep breath and hold it. Breathe in, and out. By the way, do you have a history of tuberculosis?

A：很好。現在把你的舌頭伸出來。好，接下來讓我檢查一下你的胸膛。請把襯衫扣子解開。讓我檢查你的心和肺。深呼吸，屏住氣。吸氣，吐氣。順便問一下，你曾經罹患過肺結核嗎？

B：No, definitely not.

B：沒有，從來沒有。

A：Look, your throat is inflamed. And your tongue is thickly coated. You have all the symptoms of influenza.

A：聽著，你的喉嚨發炎了。舌苔很厚。這些都是感冒的症狀。

B：What am I supposed to do then?

B：那我該怎麼做呢？

A：A good rest is all you need, and drink more water. I'll write you a prescription.

A：你需要好好休息，多喝水。我馬上幫你開藥方。

B：Thank you very much.

B：謝謝。

A：That's all right. Remember to take a good rest.

A：不客氣。記得好好休息。

B：I will. Goodbye, doctor.

B：我會的。再見，醫生。

A：Bye!

A：再見！

**Notes**

- stuff up 意思是「塞滿、填滿」。stuffed-up 此處當形容詞，指的是「（因感冒而）鼻塞的」。例如：have a stuffed-up nose 鼻子不通。
- write sb. sth./write sth. to sb. 寫某物給某人。注意：一般情況下，「寫信給某人」就用 write to sb. 來表達，當然也可以說 write a letter to sb.，只不過前者更簡潔，也是老外常用的表達方式。例如：

She's writing her friend a letter.

She's writing a letter to her friend.

She's writing to her friend.

這三句話的意思都是：她正在寫信給她的朋友。

# Unit 3 電話求助 Calling for Help

## Fresh Expressions

My house has been burglarized.

我的家被偷了。

I have just been robbed.

我被人搶劫了。

I've just returned to find that my room has been broken into.

我剛回我房間，卻發現有人進來過。

My house is on the fire.

我的房子起火了。

I was driving, and the engine cut out and it just stopped.

我正在開車，突然引擎熄火，就再也發動不起來了。

I'm calling to report a missing credit card.

我打電話報警，我的信用卡丟了。

My car can't start. Can you send somebody over?

我的車發不動。能派人來修理嗎？

My boyfriend and I was swimming at the pool. When he dove in he hit his head and it's bleeding.

我和男朋友在游泳池游泳。當他向下潛水時撞到頭部並在流血。

A bus collided with a car at the corner.

一輛公車和一輛車在街角處相撞了。

It seemed there is something wrong with my car when I was driving.

我開車時覺得我的車好像有點問題。

I'd just got out of my car, when I heard a loud crack and the fire began almost immediately.

我剛走出車子就聽到了爆炸聲，緊接著就著火了。

We will send a fire engine to your location.

我們馬上派消防車去你那邊。

Why didn't you report it earlier?

你為什麼沒有早點報案？

We'll start searching the area right now.

我們馬上就開始搜查這個地區。

We'll inform you as soon as we get any results.

一旦有結果，我們會立即通知你。

Just try to calm down, sir, and tell me where you are and what's happened.

請冷靜下來，先生，告訴我你在哪裡以及發生什麼事了。

Please don't touch anything. Our security guard will be with you soon.

請不要碰任何東西。我們的安全警衛馬上就來。

## Interactive Dialogues

### Dialogue 1

A：Hello! Fifth Street Police Station.

A：喂！這裡是第五街警察局。

B：Hello. My car was stolen last night.

B：喂，我的車子昨晚被偷了。

A：What's your name and address, please?

A：請問您的名字、地址？

B：My name is Jack Nelson, and my address is 45 Washington Street.

B：我叫傑克‧奈爾遜，然後我的地址是華盛頓街第 45 號。

A：What kind of car is it, sir?

A：先生，是哪種車？

B：It's a blue 2007 Ford Escort. The license plate number is AB1234.

B：是一輛藍色的 2007 福特護衛者。車牌號碼是 AB1234。

A：And where was it parked?

A：車子本來停在什麼地方？

B：It was parked in my driveway, in front of my house.

B：車子本來停在我家前面的車道上。

A：Can you tell me the time period when it was stolen?

A：能不能告訴我什麼時間被偷的？

B：l can tell you the time —— it was 4:20 a.m.

B：我可以告訴你被偷的時間 —— 早上 4：20。

A：Wait —— you mean you saw the perpetrators stealing the vehicle?

A：等一下 —— 你的意思是你有看到竊賊偷車嗎？

B：No, l heard them. The car alarm went off, but they must have disen-gaged it.

B：沒有，我是聽到的。防盜器響了，但他們一定把它切斷了。

A：Oh, sir, we're open all night here. Why didn't you call then?

A：哦，先生，我們整晚都在這，為何你當時不打電話來呢？

B：l was too sleepy, so I thought it was my alarm clock ringing. So I looked at the clock, reset it, and went back to sleep.

B：我太睏了，我以為是我鬧鐘在響。所以我看了看時鐘，重新設定後又繼續睡了。

A：Oh, l see. We'll send someone to your place right away.

A：哦，我明白了。我們立刻派人到你那邊。

B：Thank you. See you later.

B：謝謝，再見。

A：Goodbye.

A：再見。

**Notes**

- license plate number 車牌號碼

- driveway 馬路；汽車道

- perpetrator 做壞事者；犯罪者。例如：

  Perhaps very soon a crime with perpetrator unknown will come to light.

  或許不久就有一樁未知殺人案即將披露。

- car alarm 汽車防盜系統；汽車報警器

- go off 響起；離開；消失；昏倒；睡著；爆炸；爆發出；開始；（食品）變質；進行

- disengage 解開；解除；使脫離。例如：

  The mother gently disengaged her hand from that of the sleeping child.

  母親輕輕地把手從睡著的孩子手中抽出來。

- alarm clock 鬧鐘

- send sb. to some place 把某人送到某地。send sb. to do 派某人做某事

Dialogue 2

A：Room attendant, can you come here, please!

A：客房服務人員，請您過來一下好嗎？

B：Yes, madam. What can I do for you?

B：好的，夫人。有什麼我可以效勞的嗎？

A：My husband has slipped in the bathroom. His nose is bleeding and he cannot stand up.

A：我丈夫在浴室裡滑倒了。他鼻子流血了，站也站不起來。

B：How unfortunate! Don't worry, Mrs. Bellow. Leave it to me. (He rushes into the bathroom.) Mr. Bellow, just lean on me and I'll help you to bed.

B：多麼不幸呀！別擔心，貝洛夫人。交給我來處理。（他衝向浴室。）貝洛先生，斜靠著我，我幫您上床。

A：(Almost in tears) Go slowly though.

A：（幾乎含著眼淚）慢一點。

B：Mr. Bellow, let me pinch your nose to stop the bleeding. (Soon the nose stops bleeding.)

B：貝洛先生，讓我捏住您的鼻子，不讓它流血。（不一會兒，鼻子止血了。）

C：Oh, my goodness!

C：哦，我的天！

B：Mrs. Bellow, bring a towel and wash Mr. Bellow's face, please. Mr. Bellow, please don't blow your nose, otherwise it will bleed again. Do you feel better in this position?

B：貝洛夫人，請拿條毛巾過來洗貝洛先生的臉。貝洛先生，請不要擤鼻子，否則它又會流血的。您感覺好點了嗎？

C：Yes, but my left knee is really aching.

C：有，只是我左膝蓋很痛。

B：Everything will be all right, Mr. Bellow. I'll send for the doctor. Just relax. (The doctor confirms that it is a minor injury with no fracture or concussion.)

B：貝洛先生，一切都會好的。我去請醫生，放輕鬆。（醫生確定只是輕傷，沒有任何骨折或腦震盪。）

C：It's lucky I haven't broken my leg. I'm going to Guilin to see the beautiful scenery there.

C：真幸運我沒有摔斷腿。我就要去桂林看美麗的風景了。

B：Sure, Mr. Bellow. But all you have to do now is to take a good rest in your room. I hope you will feel better soon.

B：好啊，貝洛先生。不過您現在要做的還是在房裡好好休息。我希望您快點好起來。

A：You are most helpful. Thank you every much.

A：是您給了我們最大的幫助，非常感謝您。

B：My pleasure.

B：這是我樂意做的。

**Notes**

- lean on 逼迫；倚靠；依靠。例如：
  He always leans on others for help.
  他總是依賴別人的幫助。

- pinch 捏；擰；夾痛；軋痛；使疼痛；使苦惱；使消瘦；使感拮据；使感缺乏。例如：
  The new shoes pinch me at the toe.

新鞋太緊擠痛我的腳趾。

Her face was pinched by hunger.

她的臉因飢餓而消瘦了。

I'm pinched for money.

我手頭拮据。

- blow one's nose 擤鼻子；擦鼻涕

- minor injury 輕傷

- fracture 破裂；斷裂；折斷；骨折。例如：

  The fracture of his left leg is very serious.

  他的左腿骨折情況很嚴重。

- concussion【醫】腦震盪

# Unit 4 處理投訴 Dealing with Complaints

## Fresh Expressions

I didn't want to spend money on anger.

我不想花錢買氣受。

I want to lodge a strong complaint.

我要提出嚴重投訴。

Could you attend to this matter immediately?

你能馬上處理這件事嗎？

Would you please tell us your address, so that our manager can contact you?

是否請您留下地址，以便我們經理與您聯絡？

Thank you for telling us about it. I'll look into the matter right away.

謝謝您告訴我們。我馬上去處理這件事。

I'm sorry, madam. We'll attend to it immediately.

對不起，夫人。我們馬上就來處理。

I'm sorry, but we are glad you pointed this to us.

對不起，但很高興您向我們指出來。

I'm sorry, sir. There must be some misunderstanding.

我很抱歉，先生。這裡面一定有些許誤會。

Thank you for bringing this matter to our attention.

感謝您提醒我們注意。

## Interactive Dialogues

### Dialogue 1

A：BBG department store? I'd like to speak to your manager.

A：BBG 百貨公司嗎？我要跟你們的經理談談。

B：I'm sorry, sir, our manager is not in the shop. If you hold on a moment, I'll try to locate him.

B：對不起，先生，我們的經理不在店內。請別掛斷，我將設法跟他聯絡。

A：All right. Please hurry.

A：好。請快一點。

C：Can I help you, sir?

C：我能為您效勞嗎？

A：I've bought a stereo from your store. You've promised to deliver it on Wednesday. But I waited for a whole day and no one showed up. I called the shop, but the salesgirl was very rude. I want to lodge a strong complaint.

A：我在你們商店買了一臺立體聲音響。你們承諾在星期三送貨，但我在家等了一整天也不見個人影。打電話到貴店，卻受到了女店員的無禮對待。我要提出強烈投訴。

C：I'm extremely sorry, sir, I'll look into the matter right away. Would you please give me your name and telephone number? I'll call you back as soon as possible.

C：非常抱歉，先生，我會立刻調查此事的。請您把姓名、電話號碼告訴我好嗎？我會盡快回覆你的。

A：This is Johnson and my number is 5997422.

A：我叫強森，我的號碼是 5997422。

(Later)

（稍後）

C：This is BBG department store. May I speak to Mr. Johnson, please?

C：這是 BBG 百貨公司。請強森先生聽電話好嗎？

A：Speaking.

A：我就是。

C：Mr. Johnson, I'm sorry for the delay of delivery. It's because we have changed the schedule and the person responsible for it forgot to inform you. We have warned persons concerned, including the salesgirl on the phone. Shall we rearrange the delivery date at your convenience?

C：強森先生，對於送貨延誤一事我們感到非常抱歉。那是因為負責的同仁忘了告訴您時間有更動，我們已警告有關職員，包括電話中那位女銷售員。請讓我們另外安排一個您方便的時間送貨好嗎？

### Notes

- hold on 本意是「繼續；堅持；保持」。這裡是指「（打電話時）不要掛斷，等一會兒」。

- locate 確定……的地點（或範圍），此處是指「找出、找到」的意思。例如：

  I' m trying to locate Mr. Smith. Do you know where he is?

  我要找史密斯先生。你知道他在哪裡嗎？

- show up 出席；露面；到場。例如：

  When he eventually did show up, it was obvious to all that he had changed his original idea.

  當他最終出現時，所有的人都清楚他已經改變了他最初的想法。

- look into 在……裡查資料；深入地檢查；研究；調查。例如：

  The manager would look into the queer goings-on in the office.

  經理將調查辦公室裡發生的可疑事件。

- right away = at once 立刻、馬上。而 right now 則表示「現在、即刻」。例如：

  The storm will blow over right away.

  暴風雨很快就會平息。

  I am doing nothing right now.

  我現在沒在做什麼事。

- as...as possible 意為「盡可能……」，「越……越好」。也可以說成 as...as one can。可根據需要，在兩個 as 之間使用不同的形容詞或副詞。as soon as possible 可解釋為 very soon，意為「盡快」，也可以說成 as soon as one can。

Dialogue 2

A：What we received is not what we ordered.

A：我們收到的貨與訂購的不符。

B：Oh, we're very sorry. We will send you the correct product right away. We will also reimburse you the cost of returning the wrong merchandise.

B：哦，非常抱歉。我們將馬上把正確的貨送過去。而且我們會償付退貨的費用。

A：Our order reached us two units short. And about 10% of the merchandise was damaged on arrival.

A：送來的貨少了兩臺。到的貨大約 10%有破損。

B：We are terribly sorry. I'll have someone deliver the missing units to you and send you a replacement shipment right away.

B：非常抱歉。我馬上換批貨給您並叫人補送遺漏的臺數。

A：Will it take long? We are in urgent need of this material.

A：要等很久嗎？我們急需這種材料。

B：We'll have them rush it right through for you.

B：我們會火速把貨送給您。

A：What's more, we received the invoice, but we were charged for some things that we didn't order.

A：還有，我們收到發票，卻發現未訂的貨也被記入帳內。

B：Oh, I'm sorry. Could you please give me the invoice number and the model names of the parts ordered? We will send you a correct invoice in today's mail.

B：哦，對不起。可否請您告訴我發票的編號和所訂零件的型號名稱好嗎？我們今天會寄給您一張正確的發票。

**Notes**

- reimburse 償還；歸還；報銷。reimburse sb. sth. = reimburse sth. to sb. 賠償（退還）某人某物（金額）

- merchandise：正式用詞，指商業上銷售或商家擁有貨物的總稱。commodity：作「商品」解時是經濟學名詞，也可指日用品。goods：一般生活或商業用詞，指銷售或購入的商品。

  The shop windows are filled with foreign merchandise.

  商店櫥窗裡擺滿了外國商品。

  In Thailand rice is an important commodity for export.

  米是泰國的一項重要出口商品。

  He buys and sells leather goods.

  他買賣皮革商品。

  此外，merchandise 還可做及物動詞，意思是「促進……的銷售，推銷」。例如：

  If this product is properly merchandised, it should sell very well.

  這產品如果促銷得當，應該會很暢銷的。

- be in urgent need of 意為「急需」。例如：

  I am in urgent need of three thousand dollars and would be very much obliged if you could lend me that sum for a short time.

  我因急需 3,000 元，若您能借我此數目作短期使用，將不勝感激。

- rush through 匆忙做完，快速通過。例如：

  I'll try to rush the book through before Saturday.

  我會設法在星期六之前把這本書趕快看完。

- invoice 發票；裝貨清單

# Chapter4
## 公務事宜 Public Affairs

## Unit 1 綠色郵政 Post Office

### Fresh Expressions

Could you tell me how much it costs to send a letter by airmail from here to Singapore?

請告訴我從這裡寄航空信到新加坡要多少郵資？

Can you tell me what's wrong with this letter? It was returned to me.

我這封信被退回來了，請問有什麼問題嗎？

How long will it take to deliver a parcel to Paris by sea mail?

海運寄一個包裹到巴黎要多久時間？

What's the surcharge on this express parcel?

這個快郵包裹的額外郵資是多少？

What's the size and weight limit for mailing a package?

郵寄包裹的大小及重量限額是多少？

Do you have any mint stamps lately released for sale?

你們這裡有出售最近發行的新版郵票嗎？

I want to mail this parcel to Malaysia.

我想把這個包裹寄去馬來西亞。

I want to make this letter special delivery.

這封信我想寄限時專送。

I want to buy a few sets of commemorative stamps for my collection.

我想買幾套紀念郵票集郵用。

If you don't want it to get lost, better register it.

如果怕遺失，最好掛號郵寄。

The rates for printed matter are cheaper, but it doesn't go as quickly as ordinary mail.

印刷品的郵資比較便宜，但是不如普通郵件那麼快。

## Interactive Dialogues

### Dialogue 1

A：Good morning, is this the parcel post counter?

A：早安，這裡是寄包裹的櫃檯嗎？

B：No, the parcel post is at counter 6. It's right over there.

B：不是，寄包裹在第 6 櫃檯。在右邊那裡。

A：(To the assistant at counter 6) I'd like to send this parcel to Boston.

A：（來到第 6 櫃檯）我要寄這個包裹到波士頓。

B：What's in it, please?

B：請問包裹裡面有什麼東西？

(Opening a small parcel and showing the assistant the contents)

（打開包裹請營業員查看）

A：Just two silk scarves and a jade bracelet.

A：只有兩條絲巾和一個玉鐲。

B：All right, you can wrap it up now, and would you fill in this label and stick it on your parcel?

B：好的，您可以包起來了，是否可以請您填寫這個標籤然後貼在您的包裹上？

A：(After sealing the parcel with tape) Here you are.

A：（用膠帶封好包裹後）給你。

B：You could send such a small parcel by postal packet. It's faster that way.

B：寄這類小包裹可以用郵政快遞的方式。這樣會比較快。

A：Oh, really? How much would it be?

A：哦，是嗎？那需要多少錢？

B：$3 for every 10 grams, with a minimum charge of $20.

B：每 10 克 3 元，起價是 20 元。

A：That's certainly cheap, is there a weight limit?

A：那還不算貴，有重量限制嗎？

B：Yes, 1 kilogram. But yours is only 480 grams. That'll be $144 plus a fee of $32 if you want it registered.

B：有的，1 公斤。但您的包裹只有 480 克。需要 144 元，如果您要掛號，就要再加 32 元。

A：Yes, I would like to have it registered. It's safer that way. How much would it be by airmail?

A：是的，我想用掛號，是較安全的方式。如果航空郵寄這個包裹需要多少錢？

B：There's an additional charge of $8 for every 10 grams by airmail. So this parcel would come to about $560.

B：航空郵寄每 10 克還要再加 8 元。所以寄這個包裹約需 560 元。

A：Well, there's no need to pay that much just for a quick delivery, I'll just send it as a postal packet by ordinary mail. How much will that be again?

A：嗯，不需要只為快速郵寄支付這麼多費用。我就用普通郵寄。那要多少錢？

B：$66.

B：66 元。

A：(Handing the assistant a $100 note) Here you are.

A：（遞給營業員 100 元）給你。

B：Here's your receipt and your change.

B：這是您的收據和零錢。

A：Thank you.

A：謝謝。

### Notes

- jade bracelet 玉鐲。例如：

  It is said that the jade bracelet the princess consort wears is invaluable.

  據說王妃手上佩戴的玉鐲是價值連城的寶物。

- wrap up 裹緊；包好。但 wrap up 還可以表示成俚語的用法，意思是「收尾；結束；完結」。英文口語經常會這麼說：Let's wrap this project (work) up. 意思是我們快點把這個工作（項目）完結（收尾）吧！

- fill in 填寫；填充；填滿。fill someone in 是告訴某人一些事情（內幕、消息等），讓對方可以對事情的情況有所了解。

- minimum charge 最低費用。例如：

  The minimum charge for a banquet for 300 people is $2,700, excluding drinks.

  300 人的宴會至少 2,700 元，不包括酒水費。

■ additional charge 附加費。例如：

If the customer wishes to choose a carrier other than truck, he must bear the additional charges.

如果客戶要求選擇卡車以外的運輸工具，就必須負擔額外費用。

## Dialogue 2

A：Excuse me, is this the right counter for express mail?

A：打擾一下，這是寄快捷郵件的櫃檯嗎？

B：Yes. Is there anything I can do for you?

B：是的。我可以為你做些什麼嗎？

A：I want to send some commercial papers to New York. I was told to send them by express mail, but I know little about it. Would you be kind enough to tell me what it is?

A：我想寄一些商業文件去紐約。有人告訴我寄快捷郵件，但我對它不太了解。可以請你告訴我那是什麼嗎？

B：Certainly. Do you think your papers are quite urgent and important?

B：當然可以。你認為你的文件非常緊急且非常重要嗎？

A：Yes, it's important and urgent. I hope that they will arrive in 3 days.

A：是的，非常重要且緊急。我希望它能在 3 天內到達。

B：Oh, EMS is famous for its speed and reliability. It is, so far, the fastest international postal service available. It only takes 2 or 3 days for papers to get to New York.

B：哦，EMS 以快速和可靠著稱。迄今為止，它是最快的國際郵遞業務。文件到達紐約只需 2 至 3 天的時間。

A：Really? That's fine.

A：真的嗎？那太好了。

B：Besides, it is most reliable, for all the items are handled by a special staff and carried by a courier.

B：此外，它非常可靠，因為所有郵件都由專門工作人員處理，且由信使專門運送。

A：It sounds like an excellent service.

A：聽起來服務很不錯。

B：When we accept your mail, we'll send it to the airport by a special courier. It is received and processed by special couriers at the other end. It is then delivered by a special car to the addressee.

B：當我們接收你的郵件後，有專門信使送往機場。在那邊有專門信使接收和處理。然後有專車送往收件人。

A：Thank you. I believe I've got quite a clear idea of EMS and my commercial papers will undoubtedly go by EMS.

A：謝謝。我想我對 EMS 有一個清楚的認識了。毫無疑問，我的商業文件要用 EMS。

## Notes

- express mail 快捷郵件
- 常用於句型「Would you be kind/good enough to do sth.?」表示禮貌的請求，would 表達的語氣更委婉，比較有禮貌，表示對聽者的尊敬。

  Would you be kind enough to let us know the date of your arrival?

  請你把到達的日期告訴我們好嗎？
- courier 送遞急件（或外交信件）的信差
- at the other end 在另一頭；在另一端
- have a good idea of 清楚地了解（知道）

# Unit 2 退換商品 Exchanging and Refunding

## Fresh Expressions

I come to return this shirt.

我來退這件襯衫。

I wondered if I could return it.

我想知道能不能退掉它。

It shrank too much. Now it's too small to wear.

它縮水縮得太厲害了。現在小到無法穿了。

Can I have my money back on this radio?

這臺收音機能退錢嗎？

I'd like to exchange this sweater.

我想換一下這件運動衫。

This pair of shoes are a bit too tight. Could I change them for something bigger?

這雙鞋有點小，我能不能換一雙大一點的？

If you have the receipt, I can replace it for you.

如果您有發票，我可以給您換。

You can exchange it, provided that you haven't taken off the tag.

只要你沒有把標籤拿掉便可換貨。

I'm afraid we can't refund you after it's washed.

恐怕洗過後我們就不能給您退款了。

I'm very sorry, I can't exchange your shirt without the receipt.

很抱歉。沒有發票，我不能幫您換貨。

I'm very sorry. No refunding after it is opened.

很抱歉。打開後就不能退款了。

If it had any quality question, you can have your money back.

若品質有問題，您可以退款。

Sorry, things on sale are not allowed to be refunded or exchanged.

對不起，特價商品不能退貨及換貨。

## Interactive Dialogues

### Dialogue 1

A：Excuse me...

A：打擾一下……

B：Yes, sir. How may I be of service?

B：是的，先生。需要什麼服務嗎？

A：I would like to return this item.... Are refunds allowed?

A：我想把這個東西退掉……。可以退款嗎？

B：Certainly. The customer is always right; we are here to serve you. Is there a reason that you would like to return it? Did you have problems with our product or services?

B：當然可以。顧客總是對的，我們隨時為您服務。退掉的原因是什麼呢？您對我們的產品和服務有什麼問題嗎？

A：No, no.... It was just the wrong size.

A：不，不是的……。只是大小不合適。

B：Would you be interested in an exchange as opposed to a refund? I think I can help you to find the appropriate size.

B：那您想換貨還是要退款呢？我想我能幫您找到合適的尺寸。

A：No. I would rather just return it.

A：不用了，我還是想退掉。

B：OK. Sorry we can't give you the right one. Would you sign here for the return? We have to keep these records.

B：好的。很抱歉不能給您想要的。可否請您在這裡簽名？我們得保留這些紀錄。

A：Certainly.

A：好的。

B：Thanks. Here's your money. Is there anything else I can help you with?

B：謝謝，這是您的錢。還有什麼需要我幫忙的嗎？

A：No. Thank you very much. Bye.

A：沒有了。謝謝。再見。

B：You're welcome. Have a nice day! Bye.

B：別客氣，祝您有美好的一天！再見。

### Notes

■ be of service 有幫助，為……服務。例如：

How can be of service to you, ma'am?

女士，我可以為您服務嗎？

■ as opposed to 和……相反；與……相對比；完全不同；截然相反。例如：

I am here on business as opposed to a holiday.

我在這裡是辦公事而不是度假。

■ keep a record 意為「記錄下來；做紀錄」。keep record 意為「保持紀錄」。

Dialogue 2

A：Good morning, sir. Can I help you?

A：早安，先生，我能幫什麼忙嗎？

B：Good morning. I bought this camera here a few months ago. It has ruined two rolls of film already.

B：早安，幾個月前我買的這個照相機，已經毀壞了我兩個膠卷。

A：I'm so sorry to hear that.

A：聽您剛才說的真感到遺憾。

B：I hope you will be able to fix it or refund my money.

B：希望可以修理或退錢。

A：Have you brought the sales slip?

A：您有帶售貨單嗎？

B：Yes, here it is.

B：有，給您。

A：Sorry, sir. Your warranty was good for six months. It expired two weeks ago.

A：對不起，先生。您的保固單是半年，已經過期兩個星期了。

B：Two weeks ago? What difference does two weeks make? I'm sure it was defective when I bought it.

B：兩個星期，這有什麼關係？我敢肯定我買的時候就有問題了。

A：Er…. That could be possible. But no one can tell.

A：嗯……。那是有可能，但沒人能證明。

B：What shall I do?

B：那我怎麼辦呢？

A：Well, you can leave it here for repairing, but there will be a charge.

A：嗯，您可以把它放在這裡修理，但要收費。

B：A charge? How could that be?

B：收費？那怎麼可能呢？

A：You know that your warranty has run out. There is nothing I can do.

A：您知道您的保固期已經過了。我也沒辦法。

B：Can you make an exception in my case this time?

B：您這次能把這件事當例外處理嗎？

A：I'm terribly sorry, sir. We can't set a precedent. I hope you can understand.

A：先生，實在對不起。我們不能開這個先例，希望您能理解。

### Notes

■ two rolls of film 兩個膠卷

■ sales slip 銷貨單，銷貨發票。例如：

Goods can be exchanged only on production of the sale slip.

只要出示銷售單（發票）就可以換貨。

■ make an exception 把……當例外。例如：

We'll make an exception and reduce the price by 1%.

作為例外我們降價 1%。

■ precedent 先例。set a precedent 開……的先例。例如：

She set a precedent as the first woman executive in the company.

她開了先例當公司的首任經理。

■ without precedent 沒有先例。例如：

It is something without precedent in history.

這是史無前例。

# Unit 3 詢問匯率與利率 Inquiring about Exchange and Interest Rates

### Fresh Expressions

Tell me the current rate for TWD, please.

請告訴我臺幣的現價。

What's your selling rate for RMB yuan in Notes today?

你們今天人民幣現鈔的售價是多少？

Please wait a moment. I'll find out the exchange rate between U.S. dollars and TWD.

請等一會兒，我查一下美元對臺幣的匯率。

Today's exchange rate is 7.2 CNY against 1 U.S. dollar.

今天的匯率是 1 美元兌換 7.2 元人民幣。

The exchange rate today is 167 yen to the pound.

今天的匯率是 1 英鎊可兌 167 日圓。

The buying rate of U.S. dollar Notes is 3,209 TWD per hundred dollars.

美元現鈔買入價是 100 美元付 3,209 元。

What's the interest rate for the savings account?

儲蓄存款的利率是多少？

Please tell me what the annual interest rate is.

請告訴我年利率是多少。

Interest is paid at the rate of 1% per annum at present.

目前每年的利率是 1%。

It varies from time to time. At present it is 6%.

（年息）每個時期都不同。現在是 6%。

It allows you to earn a little interest on your money.

這可使你從存款中獲得一點利息。

The account carries interest of 4%.

該存款有 4%的利息。

The interest rate for the savings account is 4%.

儲蓄存款的利率是 4%。

The interest is added to your account every year.

每年的利息都加到你的存款中。

## Interactive Dialogues

### Dialogue 1

A：What's the exchange rate for American currency today?

A：今天美元的匯率是多少？

B：Wait a minute. I'll find out the rate of exchange between US dollars and TWD.... The exchange rate for US dollars today is NT$3,209 against US$100.

B：請稍候片刻，我來查一查美元和新臺幣之間的匯率……。今天美元的匯率是 100 美元兌 3,209 新臺幣。

A：Do you accept traveler's checks?

A：你們接受旅行支票嗎？

B：Yes, certainly. We accept traveler's checks.

B：是的，當然受理。我們接受旅行支票。

A：What's the rate for traveler's checks?

A：旅行支票的匯率是多少？

B：The rate for traveler's checks is 3,100 TWD to 100 US dollars. The traveler's service charge is two percent of the total amount.

B：旅行支票的匯率是 100 美元對 3,100 元新臺幣，旅行支票的手續費是總金額 2%。

A：By the way, how much would I get for 1 British pound sterling?

A：順便問一下，1 英鎊可以兌換多少新臺幣？

B：The exchange rate today is 36 TWD to one pound.

B：今天英鎊的匯率是 36 元新臺幣兌 1 英鎊。

A：I see. Here are the traveler's checks.

A：了解。這是旅行支票。

B：Please endorse the traveler's checks.

B：請在旅行支票背面簽字。

A：OK.

A：好的。

B：Would you please show your passport?

B：可以請你出示你的護照嗎？

A：Of course. Here it is.

A：當然。給你。

B：Thank you. You'll have it right away. How do you wish to receive your money?

B：謝謝。我馬上就還給你。你想以什麼方式收款？

A：I'd like to cash it immediately.

A：我想馬上兌現。

B：Now, Here is your money. After deducting a 2% service charge from the proceeds after conversion, the rest is 3,038 TWD. Please check it.

B：這是你的錢。扣完 2%手續費後還剩 3,038 元。請點清。

A：Right, it's 3,038 TWD. Thank you.

A：對，是 3,038 元。謝謝。

B：You're welcome.

B：不客氣。

**Notes**

- exchange rate（外匯）兌換率，匯率，匯價。例如：

Capital inflows from abroad and sharp increases in the world prices of key exports also cause the real exchange rate to appreciate.

資本從國外流入以及主要出口品的國際價格猛烈上升，也造成實際匯率提高。

- traveler's checks：即便自動櫃員機帶來「及時錢」的發展，許多旅行者仍在使用旅行支票，這在美國被廣為接受。外國遊客應確保他們以美元計價，外幣支票往往難以流通。

- cash 當「名詞」時，是「現金、現款」；當動詞時，則表示「把⋯⋯兌現」。例如：

Can you cash this check for me?

你能為我兌現這張支票嗎？

- deduct 意思是「扣除；減除」。例如：deduct a tax from one's wages 從薪資中扣稅

- service charge 意為「服務費；手續費」。例如：

Most restaurants automatically add a 10% service charge to the bill, but the surcharge often ends up in the pocket of the owner.

大多數餐廳自動在帳單裡加了 10%的服務費，但這筆額外的收入最後卻常常落入老闆手裡。

Dialogue 2

A：Sir, How much do you want to draw?

A：先生，您要領多少錢？

B：8,000, please.

B：8,000 元，謝謝。

A：I'm sorry. The code number doesn't coincide with the one you gave us when you opened your account.

A：很抱歉，密碼與您開戶時密碼不一樣。

B：I'm terribly sorry. I can't remember it exactly. Let me see. Is This number correct?

B：對不起。我想不起來了。讓我再想想，這個號碼對嗎？

A：It's correct now. Do you want to withdraw all money from your account?

A：這次對了。您想把帳戶裡的錢都領出來嗎？

B：Yes. Would you pleasure tell me my balance?

B：是的。請問我戶頭還有多少錢？

A：Yes, sir. Your balance is 11,000.

A：好的，先生。您帳戶的餘額是 11,000 元。

B：I'm sorry, but may I ask one more question?

B：對不起，我能再問個問題嗎？

A：Of course, please do. What is it?

A：當然可以。請問吧！要問什麼呢？

B：What's the interest rate for the savings account?

B：儲蓄存款利率是多少？

A：The interest on a current account is 0.72% per annum, the interest rate for a three-month deposit is 3.33% per annum, for six-month 3.78%, for one year 4.14%. You may get the detailed information from that bulletin board or our online banking.

A：活期年息為 0.72%，三個月定期利率為 3.33%，半年定期利率為 3.78%，一年定期利率為 4.14%。其他的您也可以看看那裡的布告欄，或登錄我行的網站查詢詳細的情況。

B：Many thanks. I still want to withdraw all money from the account.

B：非常感謝。我還是想把錢全領出來。

A：Sir, actually you needn't cancel your account. You can keep it for further use. In our bank, that the balance of account keeps zero is allowed. Our personal investment products are also attractive; you may buy the investment products or funds through this account in the future.

A：先生，其實您沒有必要銷戶的。您可以繼續保有以便未來之用。在我們銀行，帳戶餘額允許為零。我們的理財產品也很不錯；未來您可以用這個帳戶買理財產品或基金。

B：That's not necessary. I'm leaving here for a long time and return to my home country. Thanks, anyway.

B：不用了。我就要離開這裡回國了。謝謝您。

A：That's OK. How would you like your money?

A：好的。您想要怎樣的票面呢？

B：Can I have it all in one-hundred bills?

B：可以都換成 100 塊的嗎？

A：Of course. It'll be just a moment. Please sign your name here. Here is your money and the interest you've earned. Please check it and receive well. Wish you have a pleasant journey.

A：當然可以。請稍等。請您在這裡簽字。這是您的錢和利息。請收好點清。祝您旅途愉快。

## Notes

- coincide with 與……一致。例如：

  My ideas coincide with his.

  我的想法與他的一致。

- open an account 開戶；開銀行戶頭。close an account 銷戶

  withdraw 收回；取回；提取。賣方要從買方的帳戶提領錢用 withdrawal，買方要從銀行提領錢給賣方用 withdraw。例如：withdraw money from the bank 從銀行取款

- the interest rate 利息率；利率。例如：

  The demand deposit interest rate remains unchanged at 0.81 percent.

  活期存款利率保持不變，仍為 0.81％。

- savings account 儲蓄存款戶頭；儲蓄帳戶。例如：

  I deposit some money in my savings account.

  我把一些錢存到儲蓄存款帳戶。

- current account 現金帳戶；活期存款。例如：

  You must be 18 or above before your bank will issue a check guarantee card and checkbook as part of a current account package.

  持卡人必須要年滿 18 歲，銀行才可以發放銀行擔保卡和支票簿，來作為活期帳戶方案的一部分。

■ per annum 每年。例如：

At the present, the going rate is 3.6% per annum.

現行的年利率是 3.6％。

■ bulletin board 電子布告欄；布告牌。例如：

Bulletin board enables users to send or read messages of general interest.

電子布告欄讓使用者能傳送、閱讀大家都感興趣的訊息。

# Unit 4 兌換外幣 Foreign Currency Exchange

## Fresh Expressions

I'd like to break this 50 dollar note.

我想把這張 50 美元紙幣換開。

I'd like to know if you could change this money back into U.S. dollars for me.

我想知道能否把這筆錢兌換回美元。

Could you change these French francs for me?

能幫我兌換這些法國法郎嗎？

Can you give me 100 dollars in Swiss francs?

能否給我 100 美元的瑞士法郎？

Would you mind giving me the six pence in coppers.

麻煩給我 6 便士的銅幣。

We only offer one way change. We're not allowed to offer a full exchange.

我們只提供單向兌換服務，不能進行全面兌換。

I'd like to change these US dollars into HK dollars.

我想把這些美元兌換成港幣。

We have a change limit of 500 US dollars between 9 p.m. and 8 a.m. due to the bank business hours.

由於銀行營業時間的關係，在晚上 9 點到早上 8 點之間，我們定有 500 美元的兌換限制。

## Interactive Dialogues

### Dialogue 1

A：Good afternoon. What can I do for you, sir?

A：午安，我能為您做點什麼嗎，先生？

B：I'd like to change some money.

B：我想兌換點錢。

A：Certainly. What kind of currency have you got?

A：可以。您有什麼貨幣？

B：US dollars. What's the exchange rate today?

B：美元。今天的匯率是多少？

A：The present rate is 32 TWD to the dollar.

A：目前的匯率是 1 美元兌換 32 元。

B：Is it the same rate as the bank gives?

B：這跟銀行給的匯率是一樣的嗎？

A：Exactly the same. How much would you like to change?

A：完全一樣。您想換多少錢？

B：600 US dollars. Here you are.

B：600 美元。給您。

A：That will be 19,200 TWD. I'll make out a foreign exchange memo for you. This will only take a moment. May I have your name please?

A：共計 19,200 元。我給您開張兌換收據。只需花一點時間。請問您的大名？

B：John Smith.

B：約翰‧史密斯。

A：May I have a look at your passport?

A：我可以看一下您的護照嗎？

B：Yes, here you are.

B：好的，給您。

A：Thank you. (He gives it back after checking.) Please sign here on the exchange memo.

A：謝謝。（他檢查過後還給他。）請您在兌換收據上簽名。

B：Sure.

B：好的。

A：Mr. Smith you are exchanging 600 US dollars. Our rate is 32, which gives you 19,200 TWD. Would you like it in small bills or larger denominations?

A：史密斯先生，您要兌換 600 美元。我們的匯率是 1 美元兌換 32 元，要給您 19,200 元。您要面值小點的鈔票還是大點的？

B：I need both small bills and larger ones.

B：我兩種都要。

A：Mr. Smith, here is your money. Would you count them, and keep this exchange memo, please?

A：史密斯先生，這是您的錢。可以請您數一下，並收好這張兌換收據嗎？

B：What's the use of the memo?

B：收據有什麼作用？

A：You will be asked to produce it in order to change the TWD you might still have back to US dollars before you leave. I'm sure you know TWD cannot be taken out of the country.

A：在您離開這裡之前，若新臺幣沒用完，重新兌換成美元時您要出示它。相信您知道新臺幣是不可以被帶出國的。

B：I see. I will take good care of it.

B：我知道。我會好好保管的。

A：Thank you, and have a good day, sir.

A：謝謝您，祝您有愉快的一天，先生。

### Notes

- Here you are. 是英文口語中常用的句子，本意是「給你」或「你要的東西在這裡」，多用於別人向你要東西或借東西，你遞給他時的應答語。當給對方的東西是單數時，「Here you are.」和「Here it is.」兩者均可使用；當給對方的東西是複數時，只能用「Here you are.」。此外，當說話者給對方的東西並不是對方所指的那件物品，而是同類物品中的一個，或是說話者主動提供的物品時，就不能用「Here it is.」，而要用「Here you are.」。也就是說，「Here you are.」一般都可以代替「Here it is.」，而「Here it is.」有時則不能說成「Here you are.」。

- make out 填寫；寫出。例如：
  The teacher has made out a list of reference books.
  教師已開出了一份參考書單。

- exchange memo 兌換單。memo 便條；便籤；備忘錄

- denomination（貨幣等的）面額；（度量衡等的）單位。例如：stamps of different denominations 面額不同的郵票

- take good care of 照顧好，照料好。例如：

  Please take good care of her for my sake.

  請為了我好好照顧她。

### Dialogue 2

C：Good evening, ma'am. May I help you?

C：夫人，晚安，能為您效勞嗎？

G：Yes, I'd like to change some money, please.

G：請幫我兌換一些錢。

C：Certainly, ma'am. How much would you like to change?

C：好的，預備兌換多少呢？

G：Let me see. I'll need about six hundred US dollars.

G：我看看。我需要 600 美元左右。

C：We have a change limit of 500 US dollars between 9 p.m. and 8 a.m. due to the bank business hours.

C：由於銀行營業時間的關係，在晚上 9 點到早上 8 點之間，我們定有 500 美元的匯兌限制。

G：Well, I'll be leaving at 7:30 a.m. on an all-day tour tomorrow and I'll need at least that much. We're going to Yingge and I want to buy a lot of ceramics. I won't be anywhere near a bank. Can't you make an exception for me?

G：嗯，是這樣的，我明天上午 7 點半離開，去參加一個全天的旅行團，而我至少需要那麼多錢。我們要到鶯歌，我要買許多陶瓷製品，附近不會有銀行。你們不能為我破例一次嗎？

C：I'm afraid, ma'am, that we have to place a limit on exchange for the benefit of all our guests. If we change large amounts, our cash supply will run out and we are unable to oblige our other guests.

C：夫人，恐怕不行，為了全體顧客的利益，我們必須設定匯兌的限額。如果我們兌換大額款項，致使現金外流用罄，我們就無法服務其他客人了。

G：Well, why do you keep such a small amount in the first place?

G：嗯，你們為什麼只保留這麼小筆的款項呢？

C：We restrict the amount of cash kept at night due to security reasons.

C：我們是基於安全的理由而在晚間限定現金的額度。

G：I see. Well, I suppose it can"t be helped.

G：我懂了。那麼，我猜我是沒轍了。

C：Why don't you ask the tour guide to stop at a major branch of a bank on the way to get exchange?

C：您何不請導遊半途在銀行主要的分行停車，以便匯兌呢？

G：That's a good idea. I'll do that.

G：好主意，我會這麼做的。

---

### Notes

■ due 表示應給付或應給予某人，通常與介詞 to 連用。按照傳統語法 due to 主要引導表語，一般不引導副詞。例如：

His absence was due to the storm.

他因暴風雨而缺席。

Her success was due to her hard work.

她成功是因為她努力工作。

但是在現代英文中，due to 也可用來引導副詞。例如：

He was late due to the very heavy traffic.

由於交通擁擠他遲到了。

- in the first place 起初；本來；首先。例如：

In the first place, we should solve this problem.

首先，我們應該解決這個問題。

- oblige 做及物動詞時，表示「施恩於；答應……的請求」的意思。例如：

Please oblige me by turning down the radio.

勞駕您，請替我把收音機音量調低一些。

- oblige 做不及物動詞時，表示「施恩惠、幫忙」的意思。例如：

Will you oblige with another song?

請再唱首歌，好嗎？

- It can't be helped. 那是沒辦法的。這個句型的意思是「事情就是這樣，沒辦法了」。例如：

There's no way to change the plan. It can't be helped.

計畫沒辦法改變，只能這樣了。

# Chapter5
## 人在旅途 On the Way

## Unit 1 旅遊諮詢 Making Sightseeing Enquiries

### Fresh Expressions

I admire scenic beauty. Can you name some scenic spots?

我很喜歡美景。你能說出一些風景地點嗎？

What do you think is a must for me to see there?

你覺得那裡有什麼地方值得一遊？

Going and looking around the suburbs is a marvelous way to spend some days off.

休息日到郊外走走看看，不失為一個好方法。

You don't have to go through all the procedures. We travel agency will do all the necessary things for you.

你不需要辦這麼多手續。我們旅行社會為你安排所有必要的事情。

We recommend package tour for you.

我們向你推薦一條旅遊線路。

Do you mind travelling with a group?

你介意和旅行團一起旅遊嗎？

They will give you best suggestion to spend a holiday.

他們會提供給你度假的最佳方式。

I think a guide will tell you all about sites of interest.

我想導遊會向你介紹所有名勝古蹟的。

We have some excellent all-in holidays at very reasonable prices.

我們有一些費用全包的旅遊，價格很公道。

Hello, is there any tourist group to Las Vegas during National Day holiday?

哈囉，國慶節日期間有去拉斯維加斯的旅行團嗎？

Many people go on vacation with tour groups. But lots of people go without a group. They are called "independent travelers."

很多人跟團旅遊。但也有很多人不跟團，他們就是所謂的「自助旅遊者」。

## Interactive Dialogues

### Dialogue 1

A：Are there any tours for the Grand Canyon?

A：有到大峽谷的旅遊團嗎？

B：There are several tours of the Grand Canyon. Have you been to our Tourist Information Center?

B：到大峽谷有好幾個旅遊團。你去過我們的「旅客服務中心」嗎？

A：No, I haven't. Would you show me where that is?

A：不，沒去過。你可以告訴我在哪裡嗎？

B：Sure. It's up ahead to your left.

B：當然。往前走，在你的左邊。

A：I heard that you offer tours that actually go down into the canyon. Is that true?

A：我聽說你們旅行團真的會下去峽谷裡面。那是真的嗎？

B：Yes. It's a great way to really see the canyon. Plus, it's great exercise too, since we do a lot of hiking.

B：真的。那是真正參觀大峽谷的好方式。還有，那也是一次很好的鍛鍊，因為我們大多要靠步行。

A：That sounds fantastic, where do I go to sign up to that tour?

A：聽起來很棒，我要去哪裡報名呢？

B：Go inside the Information Center. Tell them you want to go on the tour that goes down into the canyon. You pay there. I have the next group to go down. I'll see you soon then.

B：到服務中心報名。跟他們說你要參加下到峽谷裡面的旅遊團。你在那邊付錢。我下一團就會去。那就回頭見了。

**Notes**

- canyon（既長又深，谷底常有溪流的）峽谷。例如：
  Have you been to American Grand Canyon National Park?
  你去過美國大峽谷國家公園嗎？

- sign up 意為「登記；簽約；註冊」。例如：
  If you want to come in on the project, you must sign up immediately.
  如果你想參加這個項目，你必須盡快報名。

- fantastic 在口語中經常出現，如果你常看美國電視劇，就可以注意到。意思就跟 wonderful、gorgeous 一樣，都有表示「很棒，好極了」的意思。

- go on a tour 意為「漫遊；巡迴；周遊」。例如：
  Would you care to go on a tour up to Canada?
  你想去加拿大旅行嗎？

- do a lot of hiking 多靠步行

Dialogue 2

A：Wow! What a great view!

A：哇！風景好棒啊！

B：You should see it at night. The Falls are lit up with different colored lights. It's spectacular.

B：你應該在夜間去參觀。那時瀑布亮著五顏六色的燈光。真是壯觀。

A：Really? What time does it begin?

A：真的嗎？幾點開始呢？

B：Just whenever it gets dark.

B：每當天變黑時開始。

A：Are there any walking tours?

A：有步行的旅行團嗎？

B：I know of something even better. There is a boat trip that will actually take you close to one of the falls. They give everyone rain slickers because it gets very wet on the coat. There is also a walking tour that takes you into a cave behind the falls. I recommend doing both.

B：我知道還有更好的旅行團。有一個坐遊艇的旅遊會真正帶你靠近一個瀑布。他們會給每個人一件雨衣，因為船上很溼。還有一種步行團，會帶你到瀑布後面的洞。我建議你兩樣都參加。

A：I am so excited. This is beautiful. Where do I go to sign up?

A：我好興奮呀！這太棒了！我要去哪裡報名？

B：Just go to the Information Office down there and sign up.

B：就到那一頭的「服務處」去報名。

**Notes**

- spectacular 壯觀的；壯麗的

  A leisurely walk down this trail will reward the summer visitors with solitude and spectacular scenery.

  沿著這條小道悠閒地散散步，避暑客可盡享幽靜和勝景。

- whenever 用作連詞時，意思表示「無論什麼時候；每當」。作為副詞時，意為「不論何時；每逢」。例如：

  Whenever she comes, she brings a friend.

  她每次來，都帶個朋友。

  I told him to come back whenever he wants to.

  我告訴他什麼時候想回來就回來。

- know of 知道、了解。know about 與 know of 兩者都表示知道，前者表示只是知道而已，而後者表示非常了解、熟悉。

- recommend doing sth.「建議做某事」。例如：

  I recommend going by airplane.

  我建議搭飛機去。

## Unit 2 賓館接待 At the Reception Desk

### Fresh Expressions

Let me help you with your suitcase.

讓我來幫您拿手提箱吧！

What's your room number, please? And by the way, can I have a look at your room number card?

您的房間號碼是多少？順便給我看一下您的房號卡好嗎？

May I put your suitcase by the wardrobe?

我把手提箱放在衣櫥旁邊可以嗎？

If you need something, just call me over the phone or press the button over there.

如果您有什麼需要，可用電話通知我或按那邊的按鈕。

Excuse me, here is your luggage. Please check if it is the right one.

打擾一下，這是您的行李。請查看一下是否有誤。

Would you please keep your valuables in the hotel safe?

請把貴重的東西存放在飯店的保險箱裡，好嗎？

The figures here are the charges for the meals and drinks that you had put on your tab.

這裡的數目是您記了帳的飯錢和酒錢。

Are you going to pay your bill in cash or by credit card?

您要用現金還是信用卡結帳呢？

Just a moment, please. I'll write out a receipt for you.

請稍等一下，我開一張收據給您。

## Interactive Dialogues

### Dialogue 1

A：Good morning, sir. May I help you?

A：先生，早安。能為您效勞嗎？

B：Good morning. My name is John Lucas, I have reserved a twin-bedded room for today two weeks ago.

B：早安。我叫約翰‧盧卡斯。兩星期前我預訂了一間有兩張單人床的雙人房。

A：Welcome to the hotel. Just a moment, please, Mr.Lucas. I'll get your details. (After a while) Yes, I have it. A sea view double room with bath for five nights. One thousand dollars, advance deposit paid. Is that correct?

A：歡迎光臨。請稍候，盧卡斯先生。讓我翻看一下您的資料。（過了一會兒）有了，找到了。一間海景帶浴室的雙人房，共 5 天，已預付 1,000 元訂金，對嗎？

B：Yes, that's it.

B：是的。

A：Mr.Lucas, would you please fill in the registration form for us including your name, address and nationality? Please also indicate the method of payment you prefer.

A：盧卡斯先生，可否請您填寫這張登記表格，包括您的姓名、地址和國籍？還有，請指明付款方式。

B：Method of payment? You take American Express, don't you?

B：付款方式？你們接受美國運通信用卡嗎？

A：Yes, we do. May I take an imprint of the credit card, please?

A：我們接受。我可以劃印您的信用卡嗎？

B：Why? Can I do it when I check out? I don't like giving out blank impressions.

B：為什麼？可以在結帳時再劃印嗎？我可不喜歡預印空白的印單。

A：Sorry, Mr. Lucas, we ask all our guests to do this to ensure a smooth and rapid check out. Of course, you may check the debit to your account before you sign it.

A：對不起，盧卡斯先生，我們要求所有客人都這麼做，以確保結帳

手續能順利及迅速地進行。當然，您可以先查看所有項目才簽署。

B：Well, alright. Here you are.

B：嗯，好吧！給你。

A：Thank you very much. May I have your passport, please? (The receptionist verifies the number on the record and hands it back) Thank you for waiting, sir. Here is your hotel passport and key card to Room 305. Please show it while signing bills in our restaurants. I'll call the bellboy to take you to your room. Hope you'll enjoy your stay here.

A：謝謝。我可以看看您的護照嗎？（核對紀錄資料上的護照號碼，然後交回客人）先生讓您久等了。這是您的住房證明及鑰匙卡，您的房號是 305。您在酒店內各餐廳簽帳時請出示此證，我會吩咐服務人員帶您到房間。希望您住得愉快。

## Notes

- a twin-bedded room 雙人房。例如：
  I want to reserve a twin room with bath.
  我要預訂一個帶浴室的雙人房。
- double room 雙人房（兩張單人床）
- advance deposit 訂金；預繳押金
- American Express 美國運通信用卡。美國運通公司創建於 1850 年，現已成為多元化的全球旅遊、財務及網路服務公司，提供簽帳卡及信用卡、旅行支票、旅遊、財務策劃、投資產品、保險及國際銀行服務等。
- credit card 信用卡。例如：
  Credit card makes me spend too much!
  我用信用卡，花錢總是花過頭！

- check out 結帳離開。例如：

Mrs. Hyde has checked out this morning.

海德夫人今天上午已經結帳離開。

- bellboy 行李員，旅客服務人員。例如：

Your room is 1513, the bellboy will take your luggage and show you the way.

你的房間是 1513 號，服務人員會替你提行李，帶你過去。

## Dialogue 2

A：This way, please. Room 1108 is at the end of the corridor.

A：請這邊走。1108 房間在走廊的盡頭。

B：The corridor is well-decorated, lovely!

B：走廊裝飾得真好，漂亮極了！

A：I'm glad you like it. I'm sure you'll like your room too. (unlocks the door and turns on the lights) Here we are.

A：很高興您喜歡。我相信您也會喜歡您的房間。（打開門，開了燈）我們到了。

B：I do like it. It's beautiful.

B：我真的喜歡這房間，很漂亮。

A：This room has telephone, color TV set, air conditioner, radio, mini-bar, in-house movie and international newspaper.

A：房間內有電話、彩色電視、空調、收音機、小冰箱、室內電影和國際性報刊。

B：That's great. Could you tell me something about your hotel?

B：太好了。告訴我一些有關貴飯店的情況好嗎？

A：Certainly. Our hotel has 350 guestrooms, ranging from single rooms, standard rooms to deluxe suites.

A：當然。我們飯店有 350 間客房，單人房、標準房、豪華房都有。

B：How about restaurant?

B：餐廳怎麼樣？

A：We have three spacious Chinese restaurants, a deluxe western-style restaurant, a snack gallery, large and small banquet halls, a bar and a 24-hour café.

A：我們有 3 個寬敞的中國餐廳，一個豪華的西式餐廳，一個速食廳，還有大大小小的宴會廳，一個酒吧和 24 小時服務的咖啡廳。

B：Sounds great!

B：聽起來不錯！

A：We also have conference rooms and the multi-function hall, night club, shopping arcade, business center and entertainment center.

A：我們也有會議室和多功能廳、夜店、購物部、商務中心和娛樂中心。

B：Have you got an indoor tennis court?

B：你們有室內網球場嗎？

A：Yes, it's on the first floor. And we've got a billiard room and bowling room as well.

A：有的，在一樓。我們還有撞球間和保齡球室。

B：Well, I'd like to have a brochure of your hotel, where could I get one?

B：嗯，我想要一份貴賓館的手冊，去哪裡拿呢？

A：You can take one from the Reception Desk. If you need something else, please call up the guest service center.

A：您可以去接待處拿一份。如果您還需要什麼的話，請打電話到賓客服務中心。

B：Thank you very much, indeed.

B：真是太謝謝你了。

A：Not at all. I'm always at your service.

A：別客氣，時刻為您效勞。

## Notes

- corridor 走廊；迴廊；通道。例如：

Each office opens onto the corridor.

每間辦公室的門都對著走廊。

- well-decorated 裝飾的很好的；精裝修的。例如：

In this hotel there are 168 guest rooms of various kinds, which are spacious and comfortable, well-decorated and well-equipped, with free access to broadband networks, with bath, digital television, and safe for private use, too.

酒店擁有 168 間寬敞舒適、裝飾精緻、設備先進的各類客房，所有房間均可免費寬頻上網，配有獨立淋浴間、數位電視及私人保險箱。

- in-house 內部的；存在（或起源）於機構內的；來自機構的

- deluxe suites 豪華套房。 deluxe 豪華的；高級的；奢華的。例如：

Owning 51 standard rooms, suites and deluxe suites and a combination of splendid furnishing and elegant design, the hotel ensures the comfort and convenience of every minute of your stay here.

酒店擁有 51 間標準房、套房和豪華套房、且裝潢精美，品味高雅，設備先進。您下榻的每一分鐘都備感清新、舒適。

- an indoor tennis court 室內網球場
- a billiard room 撞球間
- a bowling room 保齡球室
- brochure 小冊子；手冊。例如：a brochure on vacations abroad 國外度假指南手冊
- call up 打電話；打電話給（某人）；使人想起。例如：

  Forgive me so early to call up you please.

  請原諒我這麼早打電話給你。

  She can still call up scenes of childhood.

  她仍能想起兒時的情景。
- at one's service 為……服務；隨時提供服務

# Unit 3 觀光遊覽 Do Some Sightseeing

## Fresh Expressions

He who has never been to the Great Wall is not a true man.

不到長城非好漢。

I'd say this is the most beautiful place I've ever seen.

我要說這是我見過最美麗的地方。

It's also the largest existing imperial palace in the world today.

這也是當今世界上現存最大的皇宮。

I enjoy sleeping on the grass under the sun.

我喜歡沐浴著陽光躺在草地上。

I've never seen water so clear and blue.

我從來沒有見過如此清澈蔚藍的水。

Watching sunrise on Huangshan Mountain is a delight for passengers.

觀看黃山日出是遊客們的一件賞心樂事。

The waterfalls in the mountain provide gorgeous views.

山裡的瀑布構成了一處處美麗的景色。

These monuments are very impressive.

這些紀念碑讓人留下深刻的印象。

What a treat to get into the peace and quiet of the country.

來到這鄉間與平和寧靜的環境真是難得的樂事。

I felt as if I had been in a different word.

我覺得自己好像身處世外桃源。

Let's enjoy the beautiful view of the lake and rockery.

讓我們欣賞這美麗的湖光山色。

We enjoyed ourselves around the fire by singing and dancing.

我們圍著篝火唱歌跳舞。

The air is so warm and everything looks so fresh and green.

空氣很暖和，一切都看起來那麼新鮮翠綠。

I bet you've never seen such beautiful views before.

我打賭你從來沒有見過如此迷人的景色。

## Interactive Dialogues

### Dialogue 1

A：Uncle Ben, how did the Forbidden City get this name?

A：班叔叔，紫禁城這個名字是怎麼來的啊？

B：Well, in the feudal society, emperors had supreme power, so his residence was certainly a forbidden palace.

B：這個嘛，在封建社會，帝王擁有至高無上的權力，那他的住處當然是禁地。

A：His residence? You mean the whole palace?

A：他的住所？你是說這整個宮殿嗎？

B：Yes. The Forbidden City is divided into two parts. The southern section, or the Outer Court was for the emperor to exercise his power over the nation, and the northern part, or the Inner Court was for his royal family.

B：是的。紫禁城分為兩個部分。南部，或叫外院，是皇帝實施權力管理國家的地方，北部，或叫內院，是皇室的住所。

A：Oh, unbelievable. This was too luxurious!

A：哦，真難以置信。好奢華啊！

B：Even the whole country belonged to him. That's why he is called the emperor.

B：甚至連整個國家都是屬於他的。這就是為什麼他被稱為皇帝。

A：OK, then. I love these unique structured towers with the delicate carvings on them. It's really artistic!

A：好。嗯，我喜歡這些造型別緻的塔，它們上面有很多精緻的雕刻。真是藝術啊！

B：Yeah, the buildings and designs of the Forbidden City are the peak of Chinese traditional architecture, not only scientific but also suitable for living.

B：是的，紫禁城的建築和設計達到了中國傳統建築的頂峰，不僅科學而且很適合居住。

A：I agree. It's definitely a product of wisdom. Well, why were those small animal sculptures placed on the tops of the buildings?

Ａ：我同意。它真是智慧的成果。還有，為什麼把那些小動物的雕像放在建築物頂部呢？

Ｂ：Some of them are mascots and some are symbols of power.

Ｂ：有一些是吉祥物，還有一些則是權勢的象徵。

Ａ：Why are there so many yellow things? Is yellow the lucky color in China?

Ａ：為什麼這裡有這麼多黃色的東西啊？在中國黃色是幸運的顏色嗎？

Ｂ：Oh, no. In fact, yellow is the symbol of the royal family.

Ｂ：哦，不是的。實際上，黃色是皇族的象徵。

Ａ：Just like the pattern dragon, right?

Ａ：就像是龍的圖案，對嗎？

Ｂ：Exactly. Here is the Nine-dragon Screen.

Ｂ：沒錯。這個是九龍壁。

Ａ：Oh, it's really fabulous! I wanna take a picture here.

Ａ：哦！它真漂亮啊！我要在這裡照一張照片。

Ｂ：Sure, this will be a really good picture.

Ｂ：當然，一定會是一張很棒的照片。

## Notes

- feudal society 封建社會
- supreme power 至高無上的權力。例如：

This throne symbolized the supreme power of the feudal society.

這個寶座是封建皇權的象徵。

- be divided into 被分成;被劃分為。separate from 從……中間分離。例如:

  The house was divided into flats.

  那房屋被分隔成數間房間。

  She was separated from her husband last year.

  去年她和丈夫離婚了。

- exercise a power 行使權力。例如:

  The old man wanted to exercise his power by tormenting him a little.

  老人想要展現威風,存心折磨他。

- luxurious 奢侈的;驕奢淫逸的。例如:

  Luxurious furniture purchased here will be delivered free of charge.

  凡購買本店豪華家具,均為您免費送到家。

- mascot 吉祥物,源於法國普羅旺斯語 Mascotto,直到 19 世紀末才被正式以 Mascotte 的拼寫形式收入法文詞典,英文 Mascot 由此衍變而來,意指能帶來吉祥、好運的人、動物或東西。例如:

  The football team's mascot is a goat.

  那支足球隊的吉祥物是山羊。

- fabulous 驚人的;難以置信的。例如:

  The museum has a fabulous collection of jewels.

  該博物館有著驚人的珠寶收藏。

## Dialogue 2

A:Which city impressed you most during your trip?

A:這次旅行哪個城市讓你最難忘?

B:It was Paris, I suppose.

B:我覺得是巴黎。

A：The name of the city sounds very romantic. Tell me something about it, will you?

A：這城市的名字聽起來就覺得充滿浪漫氣息。告訴我與它有關的事，好嗎？

B：Sure. I'll begin with the Eiffel Tower first. It's the symbol of the city, you know. Hard to imagine how it was built over a hundred years ago.

B：當然好。我先從艾菲爾鐵塔講起。你知道，它是巴黎的象徵。很難想像它建於一百多年前。

A：Did you go to the top of the tower?

A：你有上到塔頂嗎？

B：You bet. I dined at a restaurant on the top platform and enjoyed the splendid view of Paris at night.

B：當然。我還在塔頂平臺的餐廳裡用餐，飽覽巴黎美妙的夜景。

A：Did you go to the Louvre Palace?

A：你有去羅浮宮嗎？

B：How could I miss it? I spent a whole day inside and still couldn't finish seeing all its collections of world-famous treasures.

B：我怎能錯過呢？我在裡面流連了一整天還是沒辦法把裡面所有聞名於世的珍藏看完。

A：What treasures?

A：什麼珍藏？

B：You must have heard about the Mona Lisa, haven't you?

B：你一定聽過蒙娜麗莎的畫像吧？

A：Yes, of course. Did you see the original painting?

A：當然聽說過。你見到原畫了？

B：Yes. And I saw the Greek statue of the Venus de Milo, too.

B：對。我還看到了希臘的維納斯雕塑。

A：The Greek goddess of love?

A：就是希臘的愛神像？

B：That's right. And of course there is the Arch of Triumph.

B：沒錯。當然我還參觀了凱旋門。

A：Is that the one that was built in Napoleon's time?

A：就是拿破崙時代建造的凱旋門？

B：Well, it was Napoleon who started building it but the arch was not completed until fifteen years after his death.

B：對，是拿破崙下令建造的，但直到拿破崙死後 15 年才竣工的。

A：Where else did you visit in Paris?

A：你還去了巴黎哪些地方？

B：I walked along the Seine River and enjoyed the views on both banks.

B：我還在塞納河畔散步，欣賞兩岸迷人的風景。

A：Did you take any pictures?

A：你有拍照嗎？

B：Yes, a great many. I'll show them to you and tell you more about my trip.

B：有，照了好多。我會展示給你看然後再跟你說多一點有關這次的旅行。

A：That's great.

A：太好了。

## Notes

- 由 impress 構成的詞組以及用法：

impress sth. on/upon sb. 使某人牢記某事。例如：

He tried to impress everything he had explained upon us.

他試圖要我們把他所解釋的內容都記住。

impress sb. with sth. 給（某人）留下深刻印象。例如：

The girl impressed her friend with her sense of humor.

這女孩的幽默感給她的朋友留下深刻的印象。

impress sth. on sb. 和 impress sb. with sth. 基本上意義相同，但前者稍有強調 sth. 的味道，後者強調 sb.。

- suppose 意為「想；認為；猜想；料想」，做插入語。例如：

You don't mind my smoking, I suppose.

我想你不會介意我抽菸。

suppose 多用於口語，是試探性的，但有一定的根據；guess 猜測性很強，缺乏依據；imagine 指「設想、想像」，與眾所周知的事實相反，強調虛構和幻想。例如：

I suppose they will leave here tomorrow.

我猜他們明天要離開這裡了。

Can you guess what I mean?

你能猜出我的意思嗎？

I imagine that you are tired.

我猜想你已經累了。

- begin with 從……開始；以……為起點；開始（做）……。例如：

Trends begin with resolute action somewhere.

潮流往往發端於果斷的行動。

to begin with 意為「首先;第一;起先;原先」。例如:

To begin with, style: it must be above all refined.

首先是風格:應該力求優雅。

■ finish doing sth. 完成某事

■ must 表示推測,其疑問部分必須與 must 後面的主要動詞相呼應。例如:

· 對現在動作或存在情況的推測:

You must know the answer to the exercise, don't you?

你一定知道這個練習的答案,是不是?

That must be your bed, isn't it?

那一定是你的床,是嗎?

· 對過去發生的動作或存在的情況的推測:

A. 表示肯定推測

a. 句中陳述部分沒有表示過去的時間副詞,這時疑問部分中的動詞就用現在完成式(haven't/hasn't + 主語)。例如:

You must have told her about it, haven't you?

你一定把這件事告訴她了,是嗎?

b. 陳述部分有表示過去的時間副詞,疑問部分的動詞就用一般過去式(didn't + 主語)。例如:

She must have read the novel last week, didn't she?

她上星期一定讀了這本小說了,是嗎?

B. 表示否定推測

表示推測時,否定式通常不是 must not,而是 can't (cannot)。例如:

He can't have been to your home; he doesn't know your address, does he?

他不可能去過你家;他不知道你的地址,是不是?

# Unit 4 文化交流 Culture Exchange

## Fresh Expressions

The culture of China is extensive and profound.

中國文化博大精深。

Confucianism is the sedimentary accretion of Chinese culture over thousands of years.

儒學是數千年中國文化的沉澱。

China needs to assimilate a good deal of foreign progressive culture, but she must not swallow anything and everything uncritically.

中國需要大量吸收外國的進步文化，但絕不能無批判地兼收並蓄。

Chinese art stresses the harmony between Man and Nature, which is an important part of China's traditional culture.

中國藝術強調人和自然的和諧，這也是中國傳統文化的重要組成部分。

TCM's contribution to the world is not only an original medical system but also a part of China's traditional culture.

中醫對世界的貢獻不僅是一種獨特的醫療體系，而且也是中國傳統文化的一部分。

Nephrite is one of China's most five famous jades. The jade culture has a long history and it is the representative of Eastern Civilization.

和田玉是中國五大名玉之一。玉文化歷史悠久，是東方文明的代表。

Martial arts do have fighting skills. At the same time, Chinese culture is deeply intertwined into it. This makes it stand apart from other fighting styles.

武術的確包括搏鬥術。同時，它與中國文化有千絲萬縷的關聯。這就

是武術和其他搏鬥方式的不同。

So it is a good way to learn Chinese culture through martial arts.

所以學習武術就是學習中國文化的一個好方式。

Red is a symbol of "Happy," "and "Lucky" in Chinese culture.

在中國文化裡，紅色代表「歡樂」和「幸運」。

The plum flowers are the symbol of grace and nobility in Chinese culture.

梅花在中國文化裡象徵高貴典雅。

## Interactive Dialogues

### Dialogue 1

A：Thank you. The tea smells good. What is it called?

A：謝謝。這茶聞起來很香。是什麼茶？

B：It is called "Tie Guanyin," belonging to oolong tea.

B：這茶叫「鐵觀音」，是烏龍茶的一種。

A：I heard of this name before. I could never understand the classification of tea.

A：我聽說過這種茶。我一直弄不清楚茶的分類。

B：The classification of tea is confusing and there is no agreement. Generally, there are four kinds of tea according to processing methods. They are green tea, black tea, oolong tea, and scented tea.

B：茶的分類是滿亂的，也沒有統一的觀點。通常，按照製作方法分為四種茶，即綠茶、紅茶、烏龍茶和花茶。

A：It is said that different tea has different benefits to human body, isn't it?

A：據說不同的茶對人體有不同的好處，是嗎？

B：Yes, it is. But there are time and personal health condition to be considered. For example, green tea is good in summer. It seems to dispel the heat and bring on a feeling of relaxation. However, it is not proper for pregnant women to drink green tea.

B：是的。但是還要考慮時節和個人身體狀況。比如，綠茶適宜在夏季喝，它似乎能驅散炎熱並帶來放鬆的感覺。然而，孕婦不適合喝綠茶。

A：There seems to be a lot of knowledge about tea.

A：關於茶好像有很多學問。

B：Of course. That's why we have "tea culture."

B：當然。這就是為什麼我們有「茶文化」的原因。

A：Tea is really useful. I was once told that it's very difficult to make tea, but I can't understand. Just put leaves in the cup and fill the cup with boiling water. After a few minutes the tea is ready. What's the catch?

A：茶真的很有用。以前有人對我說泡茶很難，但我不了解。只要把茶葉放進杯子裡，倒上開水，過幾分鐘後茶就好了。難在哪裡呢？

B：Well, what you have said is just the common case. In fact, tea drinking can be an art and learning in China. In the Dream of Red Mansion, there are over three hundred mentions of tea. And there is a chapter on how to make tea.

B：嗯，剛才你說的方法都是平常的方法。實際上，在中國喝茶可以稱為一門藝術，一門學問。在《紅樓夢》裡，茶就被提及超過 300 多次，還有一章專門講沏茶。

A：How is tea made in that book?

A：在那本書中是怎麼介紹沏茶的？

B：I don't remember clearly but it's said to take half a day.

B：我記不太清楚，但是據說要花半天。

A：Such a long time. Unimaginable.

A：這麼長時間。真不可思議。

B：It's said that it will take a long time to prepare the tea utensils and boil the water. The water is said to be important. Good tea needs good water. It had better come from the snowmelt water.

B：據說需要很長時間來準備茶具和燒水。據說水非常重要。好茶要好水才行，最好是用雪融化的水。

A：That will be hard to find in summer!

A：那在夏天是很難找到的！

B：Yes. But the procedure is much simplified now since tea has become a part of everyday life nationwide. Or else who can afford half a day for just a cup of tea?

B：是啊。不過現在因為茶已經成為普通人日常生活的一部分，過程就簡化了許多。要不然誰能花得起半天時間來喝一杯茶呢？

A：You must tell me more about tea culture in the future.

A：將來有空你一定要多跟我說些茶文化。

B：No problem.

B：沒問題。

**Notes**

- smell 透過鼻子以嗅覺去感受，聞起來怎麼樣；taste 透過嘴巴以味覺去感受，嚐起來怎麼樣。

- green tea 綠茶、black tea 紅茶、oolong tea 烏龍茶、scented tea 花茶

- hear of + sb./sth. 聽到或知道某人、某事物的情況。例如：

  I have never heard of him since he left.

  自從他離開後，我再也沒聽過他的消息。

  hear about + sth. 聽到關於某事物的消息。例如：

  I've just heard about his promotion.

  我剛剛聽到了他被升遷的消息。

  hear of 與 hear about 的意義相近，兩者都表示聽說。前者表示只是聽說知道而已，而後者表示聽說，而且是非常了解。這兩個詞組在英文中有時可以通用。

- dispel the heat 驅散炎熱

- bring on 帶來；引起；導致；提出。例如：

  The timely rain after a long time of drought will certainly bring on the crops.

  久旱之後的這場及時雨肯定會有助於作物的生長。

- a pregnant woman 孕婦

- make tea 泡茶

- What's the catch? 這句話在美劇中常會出現，意思是有什麼目的？有什麼陷阱（詭詐）？有什麼內幕（隱情）？翻譯時要根據具體語境。例如：

  This price is too incredible to believe. What's the catch?

  這價格真令人不敢相信。有什麼陷阱嗎？

- 9. the tea utensils 茶具

- 10. or else 否則；要不然。例如：

  You will stay away from my girlfriend, or else.

  離我女朋友遠點，否則要你好看。

Hurry up or else you'll be late.

快點，否則你要遲到了。

## Dialogue 2

A：Hi! Mathew. I heard there are four masterpieces of China. Have you read all of them?

A：嗨！馬修。我聽說中國有四大名著，你都讀過嗎？

B：Except the Romance of Three Kingdoms. In fact, the so-called four masterpieces are only four masterpieces of novels from relatively modern history of China. There are many more masterpieces of literature, not to mention masterpieces in other fields.

B：除了《三國演義》我都讀過。實際上，所謂的四大名著只是中國近代小說的四大名著。文學方面還有很多的名著，更別提其他領域的名著了。

A：It is the same with western culture. There are so many classics that it seems impossible to read all of them in a lifetime.

A：西方文化也是一樣的。經典名著太多了，要在一生中讀完它們似乎是不可能的。

B：There is another problem of language. You know, the ancient literary Chinese is much different from modern Chinese.

B：另外還有語言的問題。你知道，古漢語和現代漢語非常不同。

A：It is the same again! Ancient English and modern English are different. Plus there are Greek and Latin classics.

A：英文也一樣！古英文和現代英文也很不一樣。且還有希臘和羅馬語的著作。

B：So we must know our history and read those classics. What should we choose before such an ocean of books?

B：所以我們必須了解自己的歷史和閱讀那些經典名著。在浩如煙海的名著中我們應該選擇什麼樣的書呢？

A：That's really a problem. There are some books lists recommended by scholars, but there are still too much.

A：這的確是個問題。有一些學者推薦了一些書目，但似乎還是太多了。

B：I agree with you. The history is becoming longer and there are more and more classics. How about people one thousand years later?

B：我也這麼認為。隨著歷史的發展經典名著會越來越多。一千年後的人們又該怎麼辦呢？

A：We have to find a way to keep the essence of history.

A：我們必須找到延續歷史精華的方式。

B：Definitely!

B：是啊！

## Notes

■ four masterpieces of China 中國四大名著，如下：

*the Dream of Red Mansion*《紅樓夢》、*the Romance of Three Kingdoms*《三國演義》、*Journey to the West*《西遊記》、*Outlaws of the Marsh*《水滸傳》。

■ so-called 所謂的；號稱的。例如：

Her so-called friend did not offer any help.

她那所謂的朋友一點也不幫忙。

- be different from 與什麼不同；和⋯⋯不同 。例如：

  City life is very different from country life.

  都市生活和鄉村生活是非常不同的。

上篇　日常生活 Daily Life
Chapter5　人在旅途 On the Way

# 下篇
# 職場社交 Business and Social Life

## Chapter1
# 暢通求職 Smooth Job-hunting

## ▎Unit 1 打點好你自己 Dressing Up Well

### Fresh Expressions

It is especially important to make a good first impression at a job interview.

在工作面試時留下一個美好的第一印象特別重要。

It's a good idea to match your interview attire to the prospective job.

面試著裝應該適合即將從事的工作。

Shirts can go well with formal occasions.

正式場合適合穿襯衫。

Your dressing should match with the job you apply for.

你的著裝與你要應徵的工作應相符。

Generally, it's a good idea to wear a suit for a job interview.

通常情況下，穿西裝去面試是個不錯的主意。

Iron your clothing to get rid of all wrinkles.

衣服要燙，不要有皺褶。

Wear shoes that match the color of your outfit. Generally speaking, black is the best.

鞋子的顏色與衣服互相搭配。一般而言，黑色最佳。

Wear black leather shoes (wingtips or loafers) that are polished. No boots.

穿黑色皮鞋（尖頭或平底），要擦亮。不要穿靴子。

Avoid the extremes of a too elaborate or too casual style.

既不要穿太複雜的款式，也不要穿得太隨便。

Don't wear shoes that are difficult to walk in.

不要穿不好走的鞋。

Don't wear a lot of jewelry or large pieces of jewelry.

勿穿戴過多或大型的珠寶首飾。

A smile and proper clothes can be the most attractive feature, because they can light up the whole person.

微笑和適宜的著裝是最吸引人的特徵，因為它們可以讓整個人精神煥發。

## Interactive Dialogues

### Dialogue 1

A：Hi, Mary. I'm going to have a job interview next week. Could you give me some suggestions?

A：嗨，瑪麗。我下週要去參加一個面試。妳能給我一些建議嗎？

B：You need to create a good image before that.

B：你應該樹立一個好的形象。

A：It's much easier to say something than to do it. What should I do?

A：說起來容易做起來難。我該怎麼做呢？

B：For example, you should take care to appear well-groomed and modestly dressed. Avoid the extremes of a too elaborate or too casual style. This will put you on the same level as other applicants and make the interviewer consider more important qualifications.

A：舉例來說，你要儀表整齊及適度著裝。不要穿太複雜的款式，也不要穿得太隨便。這樣能讓主考官把你與其他面試者放到一起衡量，考慮一些更為重要的東西。

A：But you know I love wearing T-shirts and jeans. I really don't like dressing formally.

A：但是妳知道我愛穿 T 恤與牛仔褲。我真的不喜歡穿得正式。

B：That's just what I should remind you of it. Informal clothes as well as torn jeans and dirty shoes convey the impression that you are not serious about the job, or that you may be casual about your work as you are about your clothes.

B：這正是我要提醒你的。像磨舊的牛仔褲、髒兮兮的鞋子以及不正式的著裝會給人造成一種你對工作不認真或你對待工作的態度和對待穿著一樣不認真的印象。

A：Thank you for your advice. I know what you mean. I ought to wear right clothes at the right time.

A：謝謝妳的建議。我明白妳想表達的。我的著裝應該因時而異。

B：You've got your brain in gear. After all, clothes make the man.

B：你終於開竅了。畢竟，人靠衣裝。

## Notes

- create a good image 樹立一個好的形象
- take care to do sth. 當心／謹慎點做某事
- well-groomed 照料得無微不至的；衣著入時的；整齊乾淨的
- Clothes make the man. 佛要金裝，人要衣裝。
- You've got your brain in gear today. 你今天腦子轉得很快。

Dialogue 2

A：What do you usually wear for wok?

A：你一般工作時都穿什麼樣的衣服？

B：I don't need to face our customers too often, so usually I wear very casual clothes in my office, like jeans and a T-shirt. I feel more relaxed in that.

B：我不太面對我們的客戶，所以我在辦公室一般穿得很休閒，比如牛仔褲和 T 恤。這樣穿我覺得比較放鬆。

A：Have you heard the idea of adopting a new dress policy? It is said that what the staff wear reflects corporate values and the morale of the whole company. The dress shows work attitude too, as the saying goes, "You are what you wear." Here is one questionnaire.

A：你有聽說要開始執行新的著裝要求了嗎？員工的穿著反映了公司的價值觀和整個公司的士氣。服裝同時還反映了工作態度，如俗語所說，「你的穿著代表了你。」這裡有張調查問卷。

B：I think the rules should be set regarding what to wear on different business occasions. In my opinion, we should base our policy on what is appropriate for the day's activities.

B：我認為法規應該根據不同的商務場合穿什麼來制定。我認為，我們的著裝政策應該基於每天的具體工作來設定哪些服飾比較合適。

A：First of all, I think formal business attire should be worn when facing our customers and clients and at a scheduled meeting. That gives people a sense of credibility and authority.

A：首先，我認為見客人或客戶，以及在例會時，應該穿著正式的職業裝。這會傳遞給人們一種可信度和權威感。

B：Yes. By looking well-groomed, neat and polished, we'll be able to gain the trust of our customers.

B：是的。穿戴整齊、乾淨及優雅，我們就能贏得客戶的信任。

A：Right. But at all other times, staff can wear business casual attire. This includes casual slacks, dress shirts, collared sports shirts, sweaters or skirts. Besides these, shoes should be dress shoes or loafers; I don't think causal sandals and slipper are suitable in workplace.

A：對。但在其他時間，員工能穿休閒職業裝。這包括休閒褲、男士襯衫、有領的運動衫、毛衣或裙子。除了這些，鞋子可以是時裝鞋或平底鞋；但我不認為涼鞋及拖鞋適合在辦公室穿。

B：So we should not only write down what should be worn, we should also make clear what should not be worn in workplace.

B：所以，我們不只需要寫下什麼可以穿，且應該也要弄清楚在辦公場所哪些不可以穿。

A：The unacceptable apparel also includes: blue jeans, T-shirts, shorts, sweat suits, these are far too casual.

A：不能接受的著裝包括：牛仔褲、T 恤、短褲、運動服，這些都太休閒了。

B：I'm sorry to hear that.... The dress code maybe stifles someone's personal style or something.

B：聽到這個真遺憾……。著裝要求或許壓抑了某些人的個人著裝風格。

A：But we should know the way the staff dress at work reflects the company image, so it's actually a matter of company image, not just personal dress style.

A：但我們應該明白工作中員工所穿反映的是公司形象，所以這事關公司形象，而不僅僅是個人的著裝風格。

B：I see.

B：明白。

### Notes

■ as the saying goes 正如俗語所說。例如：

You have to look before you leap, as the saying goes.

在做事前要三思而行，正如俗語所說的那樣。

■ questionnaire（調查情況用的）問卷；（意見）調查表。例如：

It took me quite a while to fill out the questionnaire.

填寫那份問卷花了我好長一段時間。

■ on different business occasions 不同的商務場合

■ formal Business Attire 正式商務著裝

■ a scheduled meeting 例會

■ casual slacks 便褲

■ make clear 解釋清楚。例如：

Let me just make something very clear to you.

讓我向你清楚地解釋一下。

# Unit 2 職位諮詢 Enquiry about the Job Vacancy

## Fresh Expressions

I noticed that you advertised a job in this morning's paper.

我看到你們在今早的報紙上刊登的應徵廣告。

I read your advertisement and know that you have a job vacancy for an English editor.

我讀了你們的應徵廣告，得知你們需要一名英文編輯。

I'm looking for a part-time job. Is it possible to find one here?

我想找個兼職工作。這裡有空缺嗎？

I'm calling for the editor position.

我想諮詢一下編輯職位。

I saw the information about the vacancy on your company website.

我在貴公司的網站上看到應徵訊息。

Perhaps there is a position in your organization for a young, experienced, and conscientious secretary stenographer.

請問貴公司是否需要一名年輕、有經驗、認真負責的女祕書兼速記員？

Shall you need an experienced desk clerk for your hotel this summer?

貴酒店今年暑期是否需要一名有經驗的櫃檯部職員？

I saw a vacancy board outside for a teacher. Has the vacancy filled ？

我在徵人公告板上看到要招募一名教師，名額滿了嗎？

Is the position still available?

這個職位還有空缺嗎？

I'd like to know if you need any full-time secretary.

我想知道你們是否需要全職祕書。

I sent my application in a week before and I wonder if you can have an interview with me?

我在一星期前發了求職信，不知你們能否對我進行面試？

I'm very interested in that advertisement about hiring a computer program designer, and hope to know a little more about it.

我對應徵電腦程式設計人員的廣告非常感興趣，我想多了解一點。

In answer to your advertisement in today's newspaper for a secretary, I wish to tender my services.

閣下在今日的報紙上刊登應徵祕書的廣告，本人獲悉，特此應召。

## Interactive Dialogues

### Dialogue 1

A：Good morning, I'm calling to inquire about your advertisement for an English editor. I saw the information about the vacancy on your company website.

A：早安，我打電話是想詢問一下有關您們登廣告應徵一位英文編輯的事。我在貴公司的網站上看到應徵訊息。

B：yea, we need an English editor, the position is still available.

B：是的，我們需要一位英文編輯，這個位置還空缺。

A：What do you see as the priorities for someone in this position?

A：您在應徵這個職位時優先考慮哪些條件？

B：English is a must for this position, and also working experiences.

B：英文是必須的要求，還要有工作經驗。

A：I feel I am competent to meet all the requirements. Can you grant me an interview?

A：我自認有能力符合貴公司的要求。可以給我面試的機會嗎？

B：OK, Could you come…er…next Thursday about three o'clock?

B：好的 , 您能不能……下週四下午 3 點鐘左右來？

A：Well, actually four o'clock would be more convenient for me.

A：嗯，實際上下午 4 點鐘對我來說更方便些。

B：All right, four o'clock next Thursday then. The address is Green Glass Building, Government Road, and the name of the firm is Globe Office Limited.

B：那也可以，那就定在下週四 4 點鐘了。地點是政府路綠璃大樓，公司名稱是環球辦公用品有限公司。

A：Thank you very much. I'll expect to meet you at four o'clock next Thursday. Goodbye.

A：太感謝您了。我盼望下星期四下午 4 點與您會面。再見。

B：Goodbye.

B：再見。

---

**Notes**

- be calling to do sth. 透過打電話做某事

- inquire about 詢問；打聽。例如：

  I recommend that you inquire about the job.

  我建議你打聽一下這項工作。

- vacancy 空缺；空職；空額。此時 vacancy 與 available 意思相同。例如：

  We have a vacancy for a computer programmer.

  我們有一個電腦工程師缺額。

- must 作為名詞，意為「不可缺少的東西」。

- expect to do.sth. 期望做某事。例如：

  She expects to go there next week.

  她期盼下週去那裡。

  expect sb.to do sth. 盼望某人做某事。例如：

  He expects you to finish the work in time.

  他盼望你及時完成工作。

  expect + n./pron. 盼望或期待某物。例如：

  Don't expect too much of him.

  不要對他有太多期盼。

## Dialogue 2

A：International Trade Company. How can I help you?

A：這裡是國際貿易公司。有什麼可以幫您的嗎？

B：Hello, I am calling for the External Relations Commissioner position. I saw the information about the vacancy on your company website. Is it still available?

B：您好，我想就外事專員一職諮詢一下。我在您們公司的網站上看到應徵訊息。這個職位還空缺嗎？

A：Thank you for your interest. The position is still available. Have you already sent your CV to us?

A：感謝您的關注。這個職位仍然空缺。您發履歷給我們公司了嗎？

B：No. Not yet. First I want to check about the availability and see if you could give me more information.

B：不，還沒有。我想先確認是否已經招滿以及看看您能否提供給我更多訊息。

A：It is quite urgent for us to fill this position now. And I would like to stress that English is a must because of the international contacts and most likely traveling abroad very soon. If all this is not a problem for you, I recommend you to mention this, and sent to me directly.

A：現在我們很需要有人來做這個工作。我想強調的是英文很重要，因為我們需要處理國際業務且很快要去國外出差。如果語言不是問題，我建議您在求職信中提到這一點，並且直接發給我。

B：The notification period of my current job is not that long and I am quite proficient in English. I am happy with traveling abroad as I am good at dealing with people from other cultures; it makes the whole job even more interesting. I will send my resume.

B：我可以很快辭去現在的工作而且我精通英文。我喜歡去國外出差，因為我擅長與不同文化背景的人溝通；這樣的工作更有趣。我將把履歷寄給您。

---

## Notes

- most likely 是「很可能（多半、大概）」的意思。例如：
  She is the most likely girl to win the prize.
  她是最有希望得獎的女孩。

- be proficient in 熟練；精通。例如：
  We should be proficient in Chinese and English to excel, particularly in business dealings beyond our shores.
  我們必須同時精通華文和英文以便取得成功，尤其是在國外經商方面。

- be good at 善於；擅長於；在……方面（學得、做得）好。例如：

  The new secretary must know English and be good at taking dictation.

  新祕書必須懂英文，並善於速記。

  He is known to be good at trouble-shooting.

  人們都知道他擅長解決問題。

- deal with 處理；對付；安排。例如：

  I don't know how they deal with the problem.

  我不知道他們如何處理這個問題。

  （= I don't know what they do with the problem.）

  do with 常與連接代詞 what 連用，而 deal with 常與連接副詞 how 連用。

# Unit 3 應徵求職 Job-hunting Interview

## Fresh Expressions

Replying to your advertisement in today's newspaper for an administration assistant, I tender my services.

拜讀今日報紙上貴公司應徵人才的廣告，本人特此應徵行政助理一職。

I graduated from Nanjing University. My major was International Trade.

我畢業於南京大學。我的專業是國際貿易。

I suppose a strong point is that I like developing new things and ideas.

我想我的一個優點是喜歡創新。

Your company has a good reputation in this area and I heard nothing but praise about it.

貴公司在本地區聲譽很好，有口皆碑。

I prefer something in the business management for your company.

我希望在貴公司從事商業管理方面的相關工作。

I think the ideal job should make use of the professional experience I have obtained, and offer me opportunity of advancement.

我認為理想的工作應該能發揮我的專業知識，而且能為我提供發展的機會。

Shall we discuss my responsibilities with your company first? I think salary is closely related to the responsibilities of the job.

能否先談一下我在貴公司的責任？我認為薪資應該與承擔的責任密切相關。

Your firm has a great future and is conducive to the future development of my abilities.

貴公司的前途光明，有助於我的能力提升。

With my strong academic background, I am capable and competent. I think your unit needs a man like me.

憑藉我良好的學術背景，我可以勝任自己的工作，而且我認為自己很有競爭力。我想貴單位需要像我這樣的人才。

I expect to be paid according to my abilities.

我希望能根據我的能力支付薪水。

## Interactive Dialogues

### Dialogue 1

A：Tell me little about yourself, please.

A：請你簡單介紹一下你自己。

B：My name is Tom and I lived in Taipei, I was born in 1985. My major was electrical engineering.

B：我叫湯姆，住在臺北。出生於 1985 年。我的專業是電子工程。

A：What kind of personality do you think you have?

A：你認為你個性怎麼樣？

B：Well, I approach things very enthusiastically, I think, and I don't like to leave things half-done. I'm organized and extremely capable.

B：嗯，我想我做事非常熱心，我不喜歡把事情做一半。我非常有組織能力也很能幹。

A：What do you say are your weakness and strengths?

A：你的優缺點是什麼？

B：Well, I'm afraid I'm a poor speaker, however I'm fully aware of this, so I've studying how to speak in public. I suppose my strengths are I' m persistent and a fast-learner.

B：嗯，我不太擅長說話，但我已經意識到這一點，因此正在學如何在公共場合說話。我想我的優點是執著且學東西很快。

A：What made you choose this company?

A：你為什麼會選擇這家公司？

B：Your company has a very good reputation, not only because your products are of high quality, but also due to your well-constructed management system. I want to contribute to such an outstanding company which cares not only about the customers' needs, but also about the welfare of employees.

B：你們公司在業內有很好的聲譽，不僅是因為你們的產品品質很好，而且你們的管理系統也很優秀。公司既照顧顧客的利益，又兼顧員工的福利，我想在這樣優秀的企業任職。

A：Why do you consider yourself qualified for the job?

A：你為什麼認為自己適合這份工作？

B：I have the educational background and relevant experience required for the position. Besides, I am a very good team player and have the desire to succeed.

B：我有相關教育背景和工作經驗。除此之外，我有很強的團隊合作精神，而且我嚮往成功。

A：What interests you most about this job?

A：你對這份工作最感興趣的是什麼？

B：I like to work in a team and enjoy solving problems.

B：我喜歡團隊合作及共同解決問題。

**Notes**

- leave sth. half-done 表示「做事半途而廢」的意思。例如：

  He left his work half-done.

  他只把工作做了一半。

- be aware of（= realize）表示「覺察到；意識到；知道」的意思。

- qualified for 意思是「有……的資格」。對話中的句子還可以說成 Why do you feel you are qualified for this job?

Dialogue 2

A：Hello Mr. James, please have a seat. Thank you for coming in today. I have read your resume. You completed University in America?

A：你好，詹姆斯先生，請坐。謝謝你今天能來。你的履歷我已看過。你在美國完成大學學業？

B：Yes, I went to New York University. After graduation, I started right away into the advertising industry. Later, I made a bit of a switch to focus on marketing research.

B：是的，我上紐約大學。畢業後，我開始做廣告工作。後來，轉向市場調查。

A：So, what experience do you have?

A：那麼，你有什麼工作經驗？

B：I have five years marketing experience. This includes both entry level and management positions. In my last position, I worked my way up to being supervisor of the marketing department.

B：我做過 5 年市場銷售工作。包括初級職位和管理職位，並在最後的崗位上透過自己的努力當上了市場部總監。

A：I can see that from your resume. Your last position was marketing supervisor for a pharmaceutical company, is that right? Later, why did you decide to leave your former post?

A：從履歷上能看到。你最後的職位是製藥公司的市場部總監，對吧？那後來你為什麼離職？

B：I was ready for something new. I would like to have a job that is challenging, something that I can see and do new things every day. I loved many things about my former job, and I left with amiable feelings on both sides. I was just ready for something new.

B：我想嘗試新事物。我喜歡做有挑戰性的工作，喜歡每天看見新東西，做不同的工作。我很喜歡我以前的工作，而且我離開時雙方也很愉快。我之所以離開是因為想嘗試新事物。

A：I see. Do you want to work full-time or part-time?

A：我明白。那你想做全職還是兼職？

B：I would rather work full-time.

B：我比較想做全職。

A：I'll make note of that. Now, what are your salary expectations?

A：我記錄一下。你對薪資的期望是多少？

B：I am willing to negotiate, but I expect at least $60,000 per year.

B：我願意商議，但我希望每年至少有 6 萬美元的收入。

## Notes

- have a seat 表示「請坐」的意思，此外還可說 sit down；take a seat；be seated。

- amiable 意思是「親切的；和藹可親的；友好的；友善的」。例如：

  He is a most amiable fellow.

  他為人很隨和。

- work one's way 意思是「努力地做／前進」，例如：

  You must work your way through the difficulties.

  你必須努力克服這些困難。

- I would rather... 後接動詞原形，表示「寧願做某事」。例如：

  I'd rather do it without anybody's help.

  我寧願不要任何人幫助，自己做這件事。

  would rather + 從句，是一個常用的虛擬語氣句型，謂語一般用過去式來表示現在或將來。其意為「寧願……；還是……好些」、「一個人寧願另一個人做某事」。例如：

We'd rather he paid us the money tomorrow.

我們寧願他明天付給我們那筆錢。

# Unit 4 請多指教 Working for the First Day

## Fresh Expressions

Welcome to join us! I'll show you around. Come with me please.

歡迎加入我們！我帶你四處看看。請跟我來。

I hope we will become good friends.

希望我們能成為好朋友。

I hope we can work well together.

希望我們能合作愉快。

I am new here and would appreciate your guidance.

我剛來，請您多多指教。

Allow me to introduce the managing director, Mr. Liu.

請允許我向大家介紹總經理，劉先生。

Mr. Zhang is in charge of personnel and training in our company.

張先生負責我們公司的人事和員工培訓。

Welcome to our company. I hope we can cooperate happily.

歡迎來我們公司。希望我們能合作愉快。

A good beginning gets you half-way to success.

好的開始是成功的一半。

If there's anything I can do for you, let me know.

如果有什麼需要幫忙的話，儘管開口。

I will try my best to assist if you need any help.

如果需要幫忙，我會盡力的。

## Interactive Dialogues

### Dialogue 1

A：Good morning, Mr. Evans. I'm the new secretary.

A：早安，伊凡斯先生。我是新來的祕書。

B：Good morning, Miss Witt! You're a half hour early.

B：早安，魏特小姐。妳早到半個小時。

A：I don't want to make a bad impression.

A：我不希望留下不好的印象。

B：Come on over. This is your desk, and this is your time card. Be sure to clock in and out before and after you work.

B：來。這是妳的辦公桌，還有這是妳的出勤卡。每天上下班記得要打卡。

A：I will.

A：我會的。

B：One more thing. Keep your desk neat. It's the rule. There's no exception, even the art designers have to keep their desks neat.

B：還有一件事。妳的辦公桌要保持整潔。這是規定。沒有例外，既使是美術設計工作者，他們的桌子也要保持整潔。

A：I'll keep that in mind.... Does everything on this desk belong to me?

A：我會記得的⋯⋯。桌上的東西都是屬於我的嗎？

B：Not belong. You can use them as long as you work here. When you quit, you'll have to return them to the company.

B：不是屬於妳的。只要妳在這裡上班，都可以使用它們。但是離職時，妳要把它們全部歸還公司。

A：What's the extension number for my phone?

A：我的分機號碼是多少？

B：The operator will put all your calls through. You don't have to worry about that.

B：我們有總機會幫妳接所有的電話。這妳不用擔心。

A：Can I make personal phone calls during office hours?

A：上班時間我可以打私人電話嗎？

B：Of course you can. Every one has his personal matters to deal with more or less, but don't chat over the phone. What's more, don't let it hinder your work and the company's business.

B：當然可以。每個人多多少少都有私事要處理，但是別用電話聊天。還有，不要讓私事妨礙工作以及公司的業務。

A：I understand.

A：我知道。

B：When you settle down, I'll show you around and introduce you to the department managers.

B：等妳安頓好，我會帶妳參觀公司，同時也把妳介紹給各部門的經理。

**Notes**

- time card 出勤卡；計時卡；工作時間紀錄卡
- clock 作為名詞是「鐘錶」的意思，這裡的 clock 是動詞，英文的詮釋是：to record working hours with a time clock，即「以鐘錶記錄工作時刻」。例如：

We clocks in at 9 a.m. and out at 6 p.m.

我們早上 9 點上班，下午 6 點下班。

clock in and out 還可以說成「punch in and out」。

■ more or less 或多或少；有點；大約。例如：

His explanation was more or less helpful.

他的解釋多少有點幫助。

■ what's more 而且；此外；更有甚者。例如：

It's a useful Book, and what's more, not an expansive one.

這是一本有用的書，況且又不貴。

■ hinder 妨礙；阻礙。例如：

The policy will promote rather than hinder reform.

這項政策將促進而不是妨礙改革。

■ settle down 安頓下來；居住下來；安家；安定下來；冷靜下來。例如：

I want to get married and settle down.

我想結婚安頓下來。

■ show sb. around 帶某人到處參觀。例如：

I'll show you around so that you can meet everyone.

我會帶你到處看看，好讓你和大家見面。

Dialogue 2

A：Hello, friends. I'd like to introduce a new colleague to you. Her name is Jenny Chen. She will work with you from today on.

A：哈囉，朋友們。我要介紹一位新同事給你們。她叫陳珍妮。從今天起，她將與你們一起工作。

B：How do you do?

B：你們好。

CEF：How do you do? Miss Chen, welcome.

CEF：妳好，陳小姐，歡迎妳。

B：Thanks. I graduated from a university. This is the first time I have come to work in a foreign enterprise. I hope you will help me in the work.

B：謝謝大家。我大學畢業。這是我第一次在外企工作。希望在今後的工作中能多多關照。

C：Very glad to work with you, Miss Chen. I'm Jack, in charge of the office work. Oh, this is a desk for you, Miss Chen.

C：很高興與妳一起工作，陳小姐。我叫傑克，負責本辦公室工作。哦，陳小姐，這是妳的辦公桌。

B：Thank you.

B：謝謝。

EF：Very glad to know you. We will cooperate well in the work.

EF：我們很高興認識妳。相信我們一起工作會很愉快的。

B：Thank you, everyone.

B：謝謝各位。

A：Miss Chen, so this is the first day for you to work here. I hope you'll like you job.

A：陳小姐，今天是妳在這裡工作的第一天。我希望妳喜歡這項工作。

B：This is the first time for me to do this kind of work. I've got a lot to learn from you. I think I'll enjoy working with you.

B：這是我第一次做這種類型的工作。我還有很多東西要向妳學習。我想我會很喜歡和妳一起工作的。

A：I hope so, Miss Chen. Let me tell you your definite duties here. This is your desk. Please sit down here.

A：希望如此，陳小姐。讓我來告訴妳具體職責。這是妳的辦公桌，請坐這裡。

B：Thank you.

B：謝謝。

A：Miss Chen, your main duty is to answer phone calls and transfer them to the person wanted.

A：陳小姐，妳的主要職責是接電話，然後轉接給要找的人。

B：I see. What if the person wanted is out?

B：我明白了。假如要找的人不在怎麼辦？

A：In that case, you are supposed to ask the caller to leave a message.

A：如果那樣的話，妳應該請對方留言。

B：Is there anything else I should do?

B：還有其他要我做的嗎？

A：Yes, you are responsible for keeping all the files in order.

A：是的，還要負責整理文檔。

B：All right.

B：好的。

A：If you have any question, I will help you.

A：如果有什麼問題，我會幫妳。

B：Thank you, Miss Li.

B：謝謝妳，李小姐。

Notes

- in charge of「管理;看管」,表主動,主語往往是人;與之相近的詞組 in the charge of「被……管理;在……管理之下」則表示被動,主語通常是物。

  同時 in the charge of 也可用 in one's charge 形式。例如:

  I am in charge of the company when the manager is out.

  經理不在時由我來管理公司。

  This department is in the charge of Johnson.

  這個部門由強森主管。

- the person wanted 要找的人

- what if... = what would happen if... 表示「如果……怎麼樣」,不需虛擬語氣。例如:

  What if he doesn't agree?

  如果他不同意怎麼辦?

- keep sth. in order 使遵守秩序;維持秩序;使井井有條。例如:

  She likes to keep everything in good order.

  她喜歡把一切放得整整齊齊。

# Unit 5 搞好同事關係 Co-workers' Relationship

## Fresh Expressions

Jane is quite relaxed and easy-going about most things.

珍對大多數事情都很隨和。

He tends to get emotional on these occasions.

他在這些場合往往容易情感衝動。

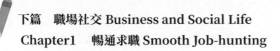

Robert's quite an extrovert.

羅伯特是個外向開朗的人。

He is quite a good man except for his quick temper.

他人滿好的就是有點急性子。

You'd better watch out, or you'll step on your boss's toes.

你最好注意一點，否則你將會得罪老闆。

I can't take the credit for this job. We all worked hard on it.

這工作我不能居功。大家都很努力。

I've received a lot of help from my colleagues.

我從同事那裡得到了不少的幫助。

We're on a first name basis.

我們很熟，互相直呼其名。

The people in your department seem so capable and nice to be around.

你們部門的人好像很能幹，也很好來往。

## Interactive Dialogues

### Dialogue 1

A：How do you get along with your co-workers?

A：你和同事的關係如何？

B：I get along pretty well with most of them. It seems there are always a few rotten apples in the bunch, though, like Margaret. I don't know why management hasn't fired her yet. She's a terrible gossip.

B：我跟大多數人都相處得不錯。不過，就像一群人中總會有些壞傢伙，比如瑪格麗特。我不知道管理部門為什麼到現在都還沒開除她。她是個可怕的八卦王。

A：Do you think management should fire someone just because they gossip?

A：你認為管理部門僅因有人說閒話就會解僱他們嗎？

B：It's not only that she gossips, but she also tries to start problems among other employees by spreading rumors and telling lies about her co-workers. She's not trustworthy, and in my opinion, I think she's nuts.

B：她不僅是說閒話而已，她還散布謠言企圖在同事間挑起事端，還對同事說謊。她這個人不可信賴，而且我認為她有點瘋。

A：So how do you develop good relationships in the office?

A：那你在辦公室是如何發展好同事關係的？

B：I think one of the important things is just to be considerate of your co-workers' feelings and needs. If you are aware of other people and do your part to make a good working environment, you should be able to get along with most of the people you work with.

B：我想最重要的事情之一是多體諒同事們的感受和需要。如果你意識到別人的存在，盡自己的力量去營造好的工作環境，那你肯定能與大多數同事相處融洽。

A：I think you're right, but it does seem that there are always a few co-workers that are harder to work with than others.

A：我想你說得很對，可是確實有些同事比其他人更難相處。

---

**Notes**

■ get along with... 與……和睦相處（= get on with）。例如：

I get along with my co-workers.

我和我同事和睦相處。

- a few rotten apples in the bunch 一群人中的幾個壞傢伙

- spreading rumors 散布謠言。例如：

  Don't blacken my name by spreading rumors.

  不要散播謠言，破壞我的名譽。

- tell a lie 說謊；撒謊。例如：

  I have never known her to tell a lie.

  我從來不知道她會說謊。

- develop good relationships 發展好關係

- be aware of 覺察到；意識到；知道。例如：

  We are fully aware of the gravity of the situation.

  我們十分清楚形勢的嚴峻性。

- do one's part 盡自己的職責。例如：

  The President asked every citizen to do his part in fighting inflation.

  總統要求每位公民盡自己的職責以對付通貨膨脹。

Dialogue 2

A：I can't stand the stupid guy any longer. It's unbelievable.

A：我再也不能忍受那個愚蠢的傢伙了。真是不可思議。

B：Oh, my dear lady, take it easy. You should forgive a green hand like him.

B：哦，親愛的女士，別放心上。妳應該原諒像他那樣的新手。

A：He does everything so mindlessly that he is going to drive me crazy.

A：他做事總是沒腦子，快把我逼瘋了。

B：I suggest you talk with him and teach him how to deal with the problems.

B：我建議妳和他談談，也教教他怎麼處理那些問題。

A：I've told him how to do that several times, but he's never listened to me.

A：我跟他說過很多次該怎麼做了，但他總是不聽我的。

B：Maybe you should communicate with him just like a friend, not a boss.

B：或許妳應該和他以朋友的身分談談，而不是上司。

A：Oh, I always have difficulty in getting along with the staff.

A：哦，我總是很難與下屬相處。

B：Just take them for your good friends and have a talk with them as we do. Make sure you won't lose your temper!

B：把他們當成妳的好朋友，跟他們討論就像我們倆一樣。確認妳不會發脾氣。

A：Oh, so bad. I'm afraid I'll change the image of myself.

A：哦，太糟了。恐怕我要改變我的形象了。

B：No, it's unnecessary. Just respect the staff and their own opinions.

B：不，不需要。只要尊重他們及他們的想法。

A：But sometimes they offer some useless proposals, it's awfully useless.

A：但有時他們會提供一些沒用的提議，非常沒用。

B：Oh, no one is perfect.

B：哦，沒人是完美的。

A：That's right. I should speak to them in a polite way.

A：沒錯。我應該對他們客氣點。

B：All men are equal in the eyes of the God. We have the equal partnership in team.

B：上帝眼裡每個人都是公平的。我們在團隊裡應該是平等的。

A：Thanks very much and you're very eloquent.

A：非常感謝，你總是說話很得體。

B：Thanks for saying that.

B：謝謝妳這樣說。

### Notes

- a green hand 生手；新手。例如：

  He is still a green hand in handling such things.

  處理這類事情，他還是個新手。

- drive sb. crazy 把某人逼得發瘋；害某人精神失常

- have difficulty trouble (in) doing sth. 意為「做某事有困難」，此句型中
  difficulty trouble 用作不可數名詞，其前可用 some, much, a little, no,
  any, little 等修飾，其後跟 in doing 詞組，in 還可省略。

  此外，還有 have difficulty trouble with sth. 這個句型，意為「某方面有
  困難」，該句式中 difficulty trouble 既可用作不可數名詞，也可用作可
  數名詞，with 後接名詞或代詞。例如：

  I have some difficulties with English pronunciation.

  我英文發音方面有些困難。

- lose one's temper 發怒、發脾氣。反義詞組為 keep one's temper，意思
  是「忍住脾氣」。例如：

  He is apt to lose his temper.

  他很容易發脾氣。

# Chapter2
## 工作交際 Office Situation

## Unit 1 要求加薪 Paying a Rise

### Fresh Expressions

My boss promised to raise my salary one month ago.

老闆一個月前說要幫我加薪。

You might get a raise if you have done an excellent job.

如果工作出色，你就會獲得加薪。

I hope to get a raise for my outstanding work last year.

我去年工作突出，希望您能幫我加薪。

You should grasp the opportunity to ask for a higher salary.

你應該抓住機會要求加薪。

I've worked here for two years and I think I deserve a raise.

我已在這裡工作兩年了，我想我應該得到加薪。

If you give me a raise, I'll take on extra responsibilities.

如果你幫我加薪，我可以承擔更多的責任。

If you work all right after one month, you will be put on the permanent pay-roll and be given a raise.

試用一個月後，若一切順利，你將轉為正式員工並加薪。

Raises will be given after three months probation period according to your performance.

3 個月的試用期後將根據工作表現加薪。

We've decided to give you three months' salary and a promotion, which includes a pay raise.

我們決定發給你 3 個月薪水的獎金並予以升遷，其中包括加薪。

All right, I'll think this over and get back to you, OK?

那好，我考慮一下這件事然後再答覆你，可以嗎？

## Interactive Dialogues

### Dialogue 1

A：Are you free, Mr. David? I want to have a talk with you.

A：大衛先生，你現在有空嗎？我想跟您談一談。

B：Sure. What's up?

B：好的。有什麼事？

A：I wanted to know why I didn't get any raise this time.

A：我想知道為什麼這次沒有給我加薪。

B：You know the company's sales are not very good recently, so there is no raise.

B：你知道最近公司的銷售不太好，所以就沒有加薪。

A：But why did other people get the raise? It's unfair.

A：但為什麼其他人都有加薪，這不公平。

B：Calm down please.

B：請冷靜一下。

A：I've been working in this company for 3 years. I did my job seriously and lots of overtime, I think you are supposed to know about it.

A：我在這公司已經 3 年了。我工作認真且很常加班，我想你應該知道。

B：I knew that.

B：這個我知道。

A：I want to be paid what I am worth.

A：我希望我的付出有所回報。

B：All right, I'll think about it again.

B：好，我會再考慮一下。

Notes

- have a talk with... 意為「與……交談」。

- What's up? 是非常口語的用法，和「How are you?」、「What's the matter?」意思一樣，是指「你怎麼樣啊？」、「最近過得如何？」、「有什麼新消息？」、「你好嗎？」

- get a raise 獲得加薪；得到加薪；漲薪資

- calm down 冷靜一點；平靜下來

  calm 主要用於氣候、海洋「風平浪靜的」，也可指人，表示「安靜的；鎮靜的」。

  peaceful 指「和平的」，表示「沒有騷擾和戰爭的」。

  quiet 指「沒有吵鬧聲的、沒有噪音的」，它強調「聲音很低、很小」或「全然無聲」。

  still 指「沒聲音的、沒動靜的」。

Dialogue 2

A：So, tell me: what makes you think we should give you a raise?

A：所以，告訴我：為什麼你認為我們應該幫你加薪？

B：I've got several good reasons. I've been here several years, my work has proven to be good, and I've noticed that people in comparable jobs get paid more than I do.

B：我有幾個很好的理由。我在這裡工作很多年了，我的工作業績很好，而且我發現做類似工作的同事薪水比我高。

A：Salaries are confidential, how do you know how much money these "other people" make?

A：薪水是保密的，你怎麼知道別人賺多少錢？

B：Well, I've noticed all the new cars around here, for one thing.

B：嗯，起碼我注意到最近這裡有很多新車。

A：Those are company cars provided to the sales staff for their business trips. Also, some employees receive sales commissions. So good salesmen will naturally earn more.

A：這是公司為銷售人員配備的公務用車。而且，某些員工得到銷售佣金。所以好的銷售人員自然應得到更多報酬。

B：That's understandable. Well, rather than comparing my salary with someone else's, perhaps we could talk about my job performance. Surely you've noticed the extra hours I've put in recently? If I were being paid an hourly wage, with the standard time-and-a-half for overtime, I'd be earning much more.

B：可以理解。嗯，不談薪資差異的話，也許我們該談談我的工作表現。最近您一定有注意到我常常加班吧？如果照時薪來算，我能得到相當於薪資 1.5 倍的加班費，我會賺更多。

A：I see your point. However, it might be hard to get a raise approved. Profits were down last quarter, and the whole company is tightening its belt, so anything that affects the annual budget is hard to get approved. But I'll tell you what I'll do, I'll give you a one-time bonus for your recent hard work. And I'll try to arrange some sort of compensation for any future overtime.

A：我明白你的意思。但是加薪的確很難。上個季度公司利潤下降，且整個公司都在緊縮開支，所以任何影響年度預算的事情都不會被考慮的。但我告訴你我會怎麼做，我會給你一次性的獎金來獎勵你最近的辛勤工作。對於以後的加班，我將盡量給予補償。

B：That would be very good of you, Mr. Green.

B：您真好，格林先生。

## Notes

- comparable 可比的；比得上的；類似的。例如：
  The music of Irving Berlin is scarcely comparable to that of Beethoven.
  歐文‧伯林的音樂很難與貝多芬的媲美。

- confidential 祕密的；機密的；表示信任的。例如：
  She spoke in a confidential tone of voice.
  她用祕密的口吻說。

- sales commissions 銷售佣金

- I see your point. 我明白你的意思；我了解你的意思。例如：
  I see your point, but I can't really agree with you.
  我明白你的觀點，但我的確不能贊同。

- tighten one's belt 忍受飢餓或貧困；勒緊褲帶；束緊腰帶度日。例如：
  In a period of mass unemployment a lot of people must learn to tighten their belts.
  在大批人失業期間，很多人不得不束緊腰帶，省吃儉用。

# Unit 2 申請升職 Applying for Promotion

## Fresh Expressions

In this company, promotion is given without fear or favor.

在這家公司，職位升遷是很公平的。

I got promoted to the manger at my business.

我被升遷為本部門經理了。

I wish to move up to higher positions.

我希望升遷到更高的職位。

I knew you were the right person to this job.

我早就知道你是這個工作的合適人選。

You did a great job last year. You just got promoted to a Program Manager.

你去年的工作很出色。你被升遷為項目經理了。

You always did such an outstanding job. Congratulations on your promotion.

你的工作表現一直很傑出。恭喜你高升。

I'm very pleased with your work. Your promotion will contribute to the development of the company.

我對你的工作很滿意。你這次升遷也會對公司的發展大有幫助。

Congratulations on your latest promotion! I know you will make good in your new job because you thrive on professionalism.

最近你升遷了，恭喜你！你的成功靠的是敬業精神，我相信你會在新的崗位上獲得更大的成就。

Let me congratulate you on your promotion.

恭賀你升遷。

## Interactive Dialogues

### Dialogue 1

A：Hi, Mark. What can I do for you?

A：嗨，馬克。我能幫你什麼忙嗎？

B：If you have a few minutes, I'd like to talk to you about my future at this company.

B：如果你有時間的話，我想跟你談談我在公司的發展前途。

A：Sure, have a seat.

A：當然，請坐。

B：Thanks.

B：謝謝。

A：Let me just grab your file. How long have you worked for us now?

A：等我把你的檔案調出來看看。你在我們這裡工作多久了？

B：I've worked here as a sales representative for about a year now.

B：我在這裡大概做了一年的銷售代表。

A：One year already? It's amazing how time flies like that. Are you enjoying your job?

A：已經有一年了啊？時間過得真快。你喜歡你的工作嗎？

B：Yes, but I'd like to have a chance at job advancement.

B：喜歡，不過我希望我能有升遷的機會。

A：I see. What job did you have in mind?

A：我明白。你心目中想要什麼職位？

B：Well, I've noticed that is a position available as a sales manager.

B：嗯，我注意到銷售部經理職位有空缺。

A：Do you understand what duties that job would entail?

A：你知道那個職務包括了哪些職責嗎？

B：Yes. I would be directly responsible for all of the sales representatives in my department. I assume there'd be more meetings, paperwork, and other responsibilities, too.

B：知道。我需要直接管理銷售部所有的銷售代表。我想大概需要承擔更多的會議、文案工作以及其他各種責任。

A：That's right. Do you have any experience in management?

A：沒錯。你有做過管理階層的相關經驗嗎？

B：Yes. In fact if you look at my resume, you can see that I was a manager before I started this job.

B：有。事實上，如果你仔細看我的履歷，就會發現我來這裡工作之前就是經理。

A：Well, I think you'd be the perfect candidate for the position. According to company policy, you'll still have to go through the formal application procedures though, so fill this application form in and I'll call you in for an interview next week.

A：嗯，我覺得你會是這個職位的最佳人選。根據公司政策，你仍需經正式申請程序，所以填好這份申請表，下週我會通知你面試。

B：Ok. Thanks for your support.

B：好的，謝謝你的支持。

**Notes**

- a sales representative 銷售代表
- job advancement 升遷的機會

■ have in mind 想要；想到。例如：

I don't know whom he has in mind for the job.

我不知道他想讓誰來做這份工作。

■ entail 必需；使承擔。例如：

This job would entail your learning how to use a computer.

這工作將需要你學會怎麼用電腦。

■ the perfect candidate 最佳人選

■ go through 經歷；仔細檢查；用完；被透過；參加；搜查；履行

■ according to 主要用來表示「根據」某學說、某書刊、某文件、某人所說等，或表示「按照」某法律、某規定、某慣例、某情況等；其後一般不接 view（看法）和 opinion（意見）這類詞，也不接表示第一人稱的代詞（me、us），例如：

According to my opinion, the film is wonderful.（×）

According to me, the film is wonderful.（×）

而要說成：In my opinion, the film is wonderful.（○）

Dialogue 2

A：I've got some great news for you!

A：我有好消息要告訴你！

B：Did you get the position you wanted?

B：得到想要的職位了嗎？

A：Yes, I'll be promoted to department manager.

A：是啊，我被升遷為部門經理了。

B：I'm glad to hear that. Congratulations!

B：很高興聽到這個消息。恭喜你！

A：Thank you. Actually, I could not believe it at first. You know, there're so many outstanding people in our company. Many of them are qualified to fill that position.

A：謝謝。其實一開始我不敢相信。你知道的，我們公司有這麼多優秀人才。很多人都可以勝任這個職位。

B：Sure, but you really did great and outperformed the others. You deserved it!

B：沒錯，但你非常出色，比他們都好。你理應升職！

A：Thank you very much.

A：謝謝。

B：You always have unique ideas and you're such a team leader.

B：你的想法總是很獨特，而且領導有方。

A：I appreciate it very much. You've been doing great. I expect to see you be promoted pretty soon.

A：謝謝誇獎。你的工作也一直都做得很好。我希望你不久後也能升遷。

B：That's very nice of you to say so. I'll try my best. When will you start at the new position?

B：很高興你這麼說。我會盡力的。你什麼時候開始新職位呢？

A：Next week.

A：下週。

B：So by then, you'll be in charge of the whole department.

B：所以到時候你就該負責整個部門的工作了。

A：Absolutely.

A：當然。

**Notes**

- be promoted to（介詞）＋職位名，意思是「被提升為」。

- outstanding 顯著的；傑出的；重要的；未解決的；未完成的；未償付的。例如：

  She is an outstanding actress.

  她是一位傑出的演員。

  The outstanding debts must be paid by the end of the month.

  未了的債務須在月底前償還。

- be qualified to do sth. 有資格做某事；有能力勝任（= having ability/ qualification to do sth.）。例如：

  She is qualified to do this job.

  她完全可以勝任此工作。

- be qualified for 有資格；符合……的資格。例如：

  Students with a background of computer programming will be qualified for this job.

  有電腦程式編寫背景的學生可以勝任這項工作。

- outperform 做得比……更好；勝過。例如：

  We're looking for ways to outperform our competitors.

  我們正在想辦法超過我們的對手。

# Unit 3 向老闆請假 Asking for a Leave

## Fresh Expressions

I'd like to take tomorrow off if that's all right with you.

我明天想請假，如果您允許的話。

I wonder if you could permit me to have one day off.

我想知道您能否允許我請一天假。

Is there any chance I take two days off?

我可以請兩天假嗎？

Do you mind if I take tomorrow off?

你介意我明天請假嗎？

I got some family issues that I need to take off tomorrow.

我家裡有點事，明天想請個假。

I caught a terrible cold last night, so I want to see a doctor.

昨晚我得了重感冒，因此想去看醫生。

I've been busy with work for a long time and need rest.

我忙了好長一段時間，需要休息一下。

It's time for me to apply for some leave.

現在該是我申請休假的時候了。

Do you think I could start my holiday a week earlier this year?

你覺得今年我能提早一週開始休假嗎？

Hope you can have two weeks of total relaxation.

希望你能在這兩個星期裡得到充分的休息。

## Interactive Dialogues

### Dialogue 1

A：Hello, this is Miss Sally of the Personal Department.

A：您好，我是人事部的莎莉。

B：Good morning, Sally. This is Tom Jones. Would you please tell Mr. Harry that I cannot attend the meeting at ten o'clock tomorrow morning?

B：早安，莎莉。我是湯姆‧瓊斯。請你告訴哈里先生我不能參加明天上午 10 點的會議，好嗎？

A：What's the matter with you?

A：你怎麼了？

B：I have a terrible headache. I must have a caught a cold.

B：我頭很痛，肯定是感冒了。

A：I'm sorry to hear that. I suggest you take a sick leave.

A：我很遺憾。我建議你請個病假。

B：Yes, that's why I'm calling. I think I won't be able to come in next two days. Could you ask for a two-day's sick leave for me?

B：對，這就是我打電話來的原因。我想我接下來 2 天都不能上班了。妳能幫我請 2 天的病假嗎？

A：Oh, sure. Please don't worry. Just take good care of yourself.

A：哦，當然可以。請別擔心。只要好好照顧自己。

B：Thank you very much, Sally. Goodbye.

B：非常感謝，莎莉。再見。

A：Goodbye.

A：再見。

**Notes**

- Would you please tell...? 這裡的 would 不是過去式，而是表示委婉的語氣。還可以說：Will you please tell...? 但沒有前者有禮貌。

- attend 表示「出席；參加」的意思，attend the meeting 意即「出席會議」。

- sick leave 表示「病假」的意思，take a sick leave 意即「請病假」。此外，請假還可以說成 ask for a leave。

- come in 在這裡是「上班」的意思，若早上要見上司，可以問他的祕書：Has Mr. Robert come in?（羅伯特先生到了嗎？）不可以說成 Has Mr. Robert returned?。

  不過，假如在辦公室裡因事外出，稍後返回；或休假後恢復上班，那就可以說 come back 或 return。例如：

- Mr. Liu will come back from lunch in half an hour.
  劉先生去吃午餐，半小時後就會回來。

- I won't come back till 8th October.
  我要到 10 月 8 日才上班。

Dialogue 2

A：Hello, it's Liu Qiang speaking.

A：喂，我是劉強。

B：Hello, Mr. Liu, this is Zhang Mei here. I wonder if it is possible for me to come in a bit late today.

B：喂，劉先生，我是張梅。我想知道我今天可否晚點到。

A：What's up? Nothing wrong, I hope.

A：怎麼了？但願沒出什麼事吧？

B：No, no. It's just my parents returning from a long trip this morning, and I'd like to go and meet them. Would you mind if I come in at 9:30?

B：沒有，沒有。我父母今天早上長途旅行回來，我想去接他們。如果我 9:30 到您不會介意吧？

A：What time are your parents coming?

A：妳的父母什麼時候到？

B：The train gets in at 8:10, it means I'd be about one hour late for work. Would that be all right? Do you think?

B：火車 8:10 進站，這意味著我要晚 1 小時上班。您覺得這樣可以嗎？

A：Well, Zhang Mei, you know this morning's meeting is very important and you must attend it. So…I mean isn't there anyone else in the family who could go?

A：嗯，張梅，妳知道今天上午的會議非常重要，妳必須要參加。所以……我的意思是妳家沒有其他人能去嗎？

B：No, I'm afraid there isn't. I'm the only one with a car. I hope you don't mind.

B：沒有，恐怕沒人能去。我們家只有我一個有汽車。我希望您不會介意。

A：All right, I suppose you'll have to go then. We'll put the meeting off to ten o'clock. Try not to be too late.

A：好，我想妳不得不去。我們會把會議推遲到 10 點。盡量別太晚。

B：Right, thank you very much. Goodbye.

B：好，非常感謝您。再見。

A：Goodbye.

A：再見。

Notes

- I wonder if...? 這是一個常見的口語句型。I wonder if/whether 意思是「我不知道可否」，其引導受詞從句，用於有禮貌的詢問。要注意的是，它的進行式形式也表示同樣的意思，但一定要用過去進行式。例如：

  I was wondering if you could come to the meeting this afternoon.

  我想知道你能否來參加今天下午的會議。

- Would (Do) you mind 後接 if 從句時，也是用來表示請求對方是否介意某人做某事。其中在「Would you mind if 從句」句型中，從句謂語常用一般過去式，也可以用一般現在式（比較少，如本對話）。而「Do you mind if 從句」句型中，從句謂語常用一般現在式。例如：

  Do you mind if I ask you a favor?

  我可以請您幫個忙嗎？

- put off 意思是「推遲；拖延；延遲」。例如：

  Don't put off till tomorrow what can be done today.

  今天可做的事不要拖到明天再做。

# Unit 4 接待工作 Reception Service

## Fresh Expressions

My pleasure, I hope your visit to Taipei is very enjoyable.

這是我的榮幸，我希望您臺北之行愉快。

You must be tired from the long flight. Please take a rest today.

長時間搭乘飛機您一定累了。今天請好好休息。

I've come to make sure that your stay in Taipei is a pleasant one.

我來是為確認你們在臺北的停留愉快。

We've arranged our schedule without any trouble.

我們已經很順利地把活動行程安排好了。

I hope my visit does not cause you too much trouble.

我希望這次來訪沒有給你們增添太多麻煩。

You're going out of your way for us, I believe.

我相信這是對我們的特殊照顧了。

We'll leave some evenings free, that is, if it is all right with you.

如果你們願意的話,我們想留幾個晚上供你們自由支配。

## Interactive Dialogues

### Dialogue 1

A:Excuse me. Are you Mr. Mike Johnson?

A:打擾了。您是邁克‧強森先生嗎?

B:Yes, I am from Northern Reflections of Canada. And are you Mr. Lin?

B:是的,我代表加拿大 Northern Reflections。您是林先生?

A:No, sir, I'm not. I'm Liu Yang, Sales Manager at ABC Trading. Hi. (extends hand first; they shake hands) Mr. Lin asked me to come and meet you, because he was unexpectedly tied up this morning. He is very eager to meet you, and sends his warmest regards.

A:不,我不是。我是劉陽,ABC 貿易公司的銷售經理。嗨。(伸手與對方握手)林先生要我來接您,因為他今早突然有事無法分身。他非常想見您,要我先代他向您致意。

B:I see. Well, it's very nice to meet you, Liu Yang. And please, feel free to call me Mike. I'm not big on formalities.

B：原來如此。嗯，非常高興認識你，劉陽。請叫我邁克就可以了。我不喜歡拘泥於禮節。

A：That would be my pleasure. Can I help you with you bags? We've got a limo waiting outside.

A：這是我的榮幸。讓我幫您提行李好嗎？我們有輛豪華轎車在外面候駕。

B：A limo? (chuckling) I see you're trying to butter me up!

B：豪華轎車？（低聲地笑）我看您們是想討好我吧！

(on their way to the hotel.)

（驅車前往飯店。）

A：I hope you had a pleasant flight over, Mike. I've travelled the trans-Pacific routes before, and I know how tiring they can be.

A：邁克，我希望您來訪旅途愉快。我以前也搭過橫渡太平洋的航線，我知道那有多累。

B：This one was uneventful, except for a little turbulence here and there. In fact, I feel as crisp as a new dollar bill.

B：除了不時氣流不穩外，一路都很順利。事實上，我覺得自己還是很有精神的。

A：Glad to hear it. Would you like an informal dinner with us tonight? Mr. Lin asked me to inquire.

A：很高興聽您這麼說。您願意今晚讓我們招待便飯嗎？林先生要我問一聲。

B：It's very nice of him, but truthfully I'd rather just spend a quiet evening in the hotel getting ready for tomorrow's appointment. Mr. Lin won't mind?

B：他太客氣了，不過事實上我更想靜靜地在飯店休息一晚，準備明天的會談。林先生不會介意吧？

A：Not at all. He expected you'd want a little rest, and rest first. Just to confirm —— you know that tomorrow's meeting is set for 10 a.m., at our office? I'll pick you up at the hotel at 9:15.

A：當然不會。他想到您可能需要稍作休息。跟您確認一下 —— 您知道明天的會議是早上 10 點在我們的辦公室舉行嗎？我會在 9 點 15 分到飯店接您。

B：That'll be fine. Liu Yang, thank you so much.

B：好的，劉陽，謝謝您。

A：It's my pleasure. By the way, are there any sights you'd like to see while you're here? I'd be happy to show you around.

A：我很樂意為您服務。對了，在停留期間，您是否想去參觀一些地方？我可以帶您逛逛。

B：Well, I have instructions not to mix pleasure with business on this trip. But could we see International Trade Center, and Zhongguancun Science & Technology Park?

B：很不巧，老闆指示我這次不能假借談公事四處遊玩。不過，我們可以到國貿中心與中關村科技園區嗎？

A：That's no problem. I'll set up appointments for later this week.

A：沒問題。這週晚點我會安排時間。

B：Thank you very much.

B：非常感謝您。

**Notes**

- tie up 繫住；使受阻。be tied up 忙碌；無法脫身；忙得不可開交

- be big on 形容對某事偏好，意思是「非常熱衷」。反義詞為「be not big on」而非「be small on」。注意介詞一定要用「on」。例如：
  Our general manager is not big on building factories overseas.
  我們總經理對到海外設置工廠不感興趣。

- limo = limousine 大型豪華轎車；大轎車

- butter up 巴結；討好；奉承；拍馬屁。例如：
  He began to butter up the director in hope of being given a better job.
  他開始奉承主任，希望得到一份更好的工作。

- be (as) crisp as a new dollar bill 這個表達十分有趣地將人的精神狀態與新鈔相比，形容「神采奕奕」。crisp 是「酥脆的」意思，用來形容嶄新鈔票，非常生動。

- mix business with pleasure 把工作和娛樂混在一起，意指「假藉公差的機會四處遊玩」。

- set up 有「安排；準備」之意，set up an appointment 等於「make/fix an appointment」。例如：
  I was hoping to set up an appointment with you for sometime this week.
  我希望和您定一下這星期什麼時間見面。

Dialogue 2

A：Good morning, you must be Mr. Mitchell.

A：早安，您一定是米切爾先生。

B：Yes, that's right.

B：是的。

A：Good. How do you do? I'm Jonathan Browning. Welcome to Taipei. How was your flight over?

A：太好了。您好，我是喬納森‧布朗寧。歡迎來臺北。您的整個飛行旅途如何呢？

B：The flight was all right, thank you.

B：很好，謝謝。

A：Is this your first time to visit our country?

A：這是您第一次到我國嗎？

B：Oh, no. I have already made several trips to Kaohsiung. This is my first trip to Taipei, though. It's a lot larger than I expected it would be.

B：哦，不是。我之前去過高雄幾次。不過，這是我第一次來臺北。臺北比我想像得大多了。

A：Yes, Taipei has grown considerably over the last few years. What would you like to see while you are here?

A：是的，臺北在最近幾年發展迅速。您在駐留期間想去哪裡看看嗎？

B：I hope to have time to visit the Taipei 101 while I am here. I have always wanted to go there. I think it would be a real shame if I came all the way to Taipei and make it out to the Taipei 101. Do you think I will have a chance to see it?

B：我希望有時間參觀一下臺北 101。我一直想去那裡。我遠道來臺北，如果沒有去遊覽臺北 101 的話，我想我會非常遺憾的。你認為我有機會去參觀嗎？

A：I'm pretty sure it can be arranged. The Taipei 101 is a short distance from the city, and we can make arrangements with the driver to take us out to visit the Taipei 101 during one of our afternoon breaks. I also recommend you visit Nation Palace Museum while you're at it.

A：我非常確定可以安排。臺北 101 離市區不遠，我們可以跟司機商量一下找個下午休息的時間帶您去看看。我還建議您順便遊覽一下故宮。

B：Yes, that would be nice. Will I have a tour guide to accompany me to these places?

B：好，那太棒了。參觀這些地方有導遊陪嗎？

A：Don't worry, I will be able to go along with you. Over the next few days, if you have any questions or problems, I will be right here to help you out. I am glad to be your translator and tour guide.

A：別擔心，我會一直跟著您。在接下來的幾天裡，如果您有什麼疑問和困難，我會幫您解決。我樂意當您的翻譯和導遊。

B：Thank you very much!

B：太謝謝你了！

A：My pleasure, I hope your visit to Taipei is very enjoyable.

A：這是我的榮幸，我希望您臺北之行愉快。

### Notes

- be a real shame 非常遺憾。例如：
  It's a real shame we have to give up the chance.
  我們必須放棄機會，真是可惜。

- come all the way 專程造訪；遠道而來。例如：
  He come all the way from America.
  他從美國遠道而來。

■ accompany sb. to someplace 陪同……去。例如：

He insisted on accompanying her to go to the station.

他堅持要陪她去車站。

■ go along with 陪同前往；隨行。例如：

He was too shrewd to go along with them on a road that could lead only to their overthrow.

他很精明沒有跟他們順著這條路走下去，因為這條路只會把他們引向垮臺的方向。

■ help sb. out 幫助某人解決難題；幫助某人擺脫困境；幫助某人完成工作。例如：

I can't work out this math problem. Please help me out.

我無法解出這道數學題。請幫我解決。

# Unit 5 電話找人 Call in Someone

### Fresh Expressions

May I speak to Linda, please?

我要找琳達講話，可以嗎？

Do you know his room number?

你知道他的房間號嗎？

Could you take a message for me, please?

你能幫我留個訊息嗎？

Could you give me some ideas when he'll be back?

你能告訴我他什麼時候回來嗎？

I'm trying to reach someone who is staying in your hotel.

我正想辦法與你們旅館的一位客人聯繫。

Would you mind holding a minute while I try to find him?

你可以稍等一會兒讓我去找他嗎？

Let me check and see if he's available.

讓我去看看他在不在。

I'm not quite sure about that. Can I call you back in a few minutes?

我不是很確定。我可以幾分鐘後再打給你嗎？

Would you mind calling back later?/Could you call back later?

您能待會再打嗎？

The line's engaged. Will you hold?

電話滿線。您要等嗎？

I'll ask him to call you as soon as he's back.

他一回來，我就叫他打電話給您。

## Interactive Dialogues

### Dialogue 1

A：Hello. This is the Star.

A：喂。這裡是星報。

B：May I speak with Mr. David Parrot?

B：請大衛‧帕雷特先生聽電話好嗎？

A：Who's speaking please?

A：請問您是哪一位？

B：This is Norah Sweet.

B：我是諾娜‧斯威特。

A：All right. I'll call him for you. (Speaking to David) Dave, here's a call for you from Miss Sweet.

A：好的。我替您叫他。（對大衛講話）戴夫（大衛的暱稱），斯威特小姐打電話給你。

C：Thanks. (Speaking into the phone) Hello, this is Dave.

C：謝謝。（對著電話）喂，我是戴夫。

B：Oh, hello, Dave. How are you?

B：哦，喂，戴夫。你好嗎？

C：Fine, thanks. What's up?

C：很好，謝謝。怎麼了嗎？

B：I'm passing by your office. I wonder if I can drop by.

B：我路過你的辦公室。我想知道我可否進去。

C：Sure. Where are you calling from?

C：當然可以。妳在哪裡打電話？

B：Just Nearby.

B：就在附近。

C：Hm, hm. Come over to the receptionist's desk and call me from three. I'll get through in a few minutes.

C：嗯，嗯。到接待處來，到了那裡再打給我。我幾分鐘就到了。

B：That's fine. I'll see you later then.

B：好的。那一會兒見。

C：Goodbye for now.

C：再見。

**Notes**

- speak with sb. 與某人講話。例如：

Rose spoke with Peter just now.

Rose 剛剛與 Peter 講過話。

speak about sth. 談論某事物或某事。例如：

They are speaking about a new movie.

他們正在談論一部新電影。

speak with 與 speak to 都含有與某人說話的意思，但是 with 一般帶有互動交流的意思，而 to 則著重指動作執行者有交流意願。

- pass by 經過；路過。例如：

A bus has just passed by.

一輛公車剛剛經過。

- drop by 順便拜訪；順道拜訪；非正式訪問。例如：

Would you drop by when you are in town?

你來城裡就順道來玩好嗎？

- get through 完成；到達；度過；用光；（使人）明白；透過；接通（電話）

Dialogue 2

A：Good morning. DHN Company. How can I help you?

A：早安。這裡是 DHN 公司。我能為您提供什麼幫助嗎？

B：Hello, this is John White from ABC Company. Could I speak to Jane, please?

B：您好，我是 ABC 公司的約翰‧懷特。可以讓珍接電話嗎？

A：Just a moment, please.

A：請稍等。

B：I have John White on the line for you.

B：有個叫約翰‧懷特的人打電話找您。

C：Thank you. Hi, John. Nice to hear from you. How's the American weather?

C：謝謝。你好，約翰，接到你的電話真高興。美國那邊的天氣怎麼樣？

B：It's pretty good for the time of year. What's it like in Taiwan?

B：四季中的這時還不錯。臺灣那邊的天氣呢？

C：It's fine.

C：很好。

B：That's great because I'm planning to come across next month.

B：那太好了，我打算下個月過去一趟。

C：Really? Well, you'll come by to see us while you're here, I hope!

C：真的嗎？嗯，那麼我希望你來時能順便過來看看我們！

B：That's what I'm phoning about. I've got a meeting with a customer in Taipei on next month. I was hoping we could arrange to meet up either before or after.

B：這正是我打電話想要說的事情。我下個月要在臺北會見一個客戶。我希望在那之前或之後我們能找個時間見面。

C：Great. That would give us a chance to show you the convention centre where Helen has arranged your reception.

C：太好了。那樣我們就有機會帶你參觀一下會議中心了，海倫已在那為你安排了接待活動。

B：That's what I was thinking.

B：我也是那麼想的。

C：When will you arrive in Taipei?

C：你什麼時候到臺北？

B：I'm not sure.

B：還沒定好。

C：Look, why don't you fax me your information once you've confirmed your flight time? Then we'll get back to you with an itinerary for the day, right?

C：聽著，何不等你確定航班日期時傳真告訴我資訊呢？那樣我們就可以回覆給你當天的行程安排，可以嗎？

B：That's right. Good, well, I'll do that and look forward to seeing you next month.

B：對啊。好，我會這麼做並期待下個月與你們的見面。

C：Same here. See you next month.

C：我也是，那就下個月見。

**Notes**

- on the line 在線上。例如：

  It's your friend on the line.

  是你的朋友打來的電話。

- come by 從旁走過；得到；順便過來

- look forward to doing sth. 盼望著做某事。例如：

  We are looking forward to receiving his letter.

  我們盼望收到他的回信。

- same here 意思是「我也是」、「彼此彼此，我也一樣」或「我的意見與你相同」。

# Unit 6 留個口信 Leaving a Message

## Fresh Expressions

Can I leave him a voice mail?

我可以留言嗎？

I'll just leave a message on her answering machine.

我會在她的答錄機留話。

May I leave a message?

我可以留言嗎？

May I take a message?

你要不要留話？

Can I take a message?

我可以給他留個訊息嗎？

Would you like to leave a message on his voice mail, then?

你要不要在他的語音信箱裡留言？

Would you like to be transferred into her voice mail?

你要我幫你轉到她的答錄機嗎？

I wonder if you could give Mr. Wang a message for me?

你能不能幫我留個訊息給王先生？

Could you ask him to call me at the Hilton Hotel, Room No. 654?

請轉告他打電話到希爾頓飯店 654 號房來找我，好嗎？

Please have her return my call. She has my number.

請她回電話給我。她知道我的號碼。

I will be happy to pass along your message to my boss.

我很樂意轉達您的留言給我們老闆。

## Interactive Dialogues

### Dialogue 1

A：Hello. This is Jim Brown of the Export Department. May I speak to Mr. Wang?

A：喂。我是出口部的吉米‧布朗，我可以跟王先生說話嗎？

B：I'm sorry, but he is out of the office right now.

B：抱歉，但他現在不在辦公室。

A：When will he be back?

A：他什麼時候會回來呢？

B：He should be back at any moment.

B：他應該隨時都會回來。

A：I wonder if you could give Mr. Wang a message for me?

A：你能不能幫我留個訊息給王先生？

B：Yes, certainly. Just a minute. I'll get a pen. (Pause) Okay, please carry on.

B：可以，當然。請等一下，我拿支筆。（暫停）好了，請說。

A：There will be a very urgent meeting at three o'clock and I would like Mr. Wang to attend it.

A：3 點有個緊急會議，我想要王先生參加。

B：OKay, an urgent meeting…three o'clock…. May I ask what it's regarding?

B：好的，緊急會議……3 點……。可以問一下是關於什麼方面的嗎？

A：Yes. It's regarding the foreign exchange market and our sales strategy this year.

A：可以。它是關於今年外匯市場和我們的銷售策略。

B：Shall I tell Mr. Wang to prepare any material?

B：我要告訴王先生準備一些資料嗎？

A：Yes, thank you.

A：是的，謝謝你。

B：I'll let him know, Mr. Brown.

B：我會告訴他的，布朗先生。

A：Thank you very much. Bye.

A：非常感謝。再見。

B：Bye.

B：再見。

## Notes

- Sorry, but... 是用於致歉時的客套話。先說 Sorry 表示有困難，顯得周到有禮，接著在 but 之後，再說明狀況。

- 表達「他不在，要留話嗎？」這種意思的表達法有以下幾種：

  He is not in now. May I take a message?

  He is out at the moment. Would you like to leave a message?

  He is not available right now. May I give him a message for you?

  He is away from his desk. Can I take a message?

  這句話適用於「某人」只是暫時不在，但仍然會回來時。請對方留話即表示自己將告知「某人」，請其主動聯絡，而不必勞煩對方再打來。「may」是用於請求或徵詢時的助動詞，亦可用「can」代替，不過「may」在語氣上較為客氣。

- let sb. know 告訴；通知；讓某人知道

Dialogue 2

A：Good morning, the Taipei Hotel. Can I help you?

A：早安，這裡是臺北旅館。要我效勞嗎？

B：Good morning! I'm trying to reach someone who is staying in your hotel.

B：早安！我正想辦法與您們旅館的一位客人聯繫。

A：What is that person's name?

A：他叫什麼名字？

B：Tom Smith.

B：湯姆·史密斯。

A：Do you know his room number?

A：您知道他的房間號碼嗎？

B：No, l don't.

B：不，我不知道。

A：Hold on, please. I'll put you through.

A：請不要掛斷。我將幫您接通。

(Pause)

（暫停）

A：I'm sorry there is no answer. Would you like to leave a message or to call back?

A：對不起，沒人接。您要過一會兒再打還是留個訊息呢？

B：I'll leave a message.

B：我要留個訊息。

A：Hold on, please. I'll put you through to the Reception.

A：請不要掛斷。我幫您接通接待處。

(Pause)

（暫停）

C：Good morning! Reception. May I help you?

C：早安！這裡是接待處。要我為您效勞嗎？

B：l tried to contact Mr. Tom Smith staying in your hotel, but he was not in his room. Could you take a message for him, please?

B：我想與您們旅館的住客湯姆‧史密斯聯繫，但他不在房間。您能幫我留個訊息給他嗎？

C：Certainly, sir. For Mr. Tom Smith from New York?

C：當然可以，先生。是從紐約來的湯姆‧史密斯嗎？

B：Yes.

B：是的。

C：May I know who's calling, please?

C：可以告訴我您是誰嗎？

B：Yes. My name is Kevin Black. Could you ask him to call me back as soon as he arrives at the hotel, my telephone number is 5589712.

B：可以。我叫凱文‧布萊克。請您告訴他一到旅館就打電話給我好嗎？我的電話號碼是 5589712。

C：Is that the message?

C：就這些嗎？

B：Yes, that's all.

B：是的，就這些。

C：l will repeat your message. The message is for Mr. Tom Smith from Mr. Kevin Black: Please call him back at 5589712 when you arrive at the hotel, is that coned?

C：我重複一下您的留言。這個訊息來自凱文‧布萊克給湯姆‧史密斯：到達旅館後請打 5589712 與他聯絡，對嗎？

B：That's right. Thank you.

B：對。謝謝您。

C：You're welcome.

C：別客氣。

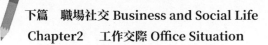

- try to reach someone 設法與某人取得聯繫

- leave a message 留個訊息。take a message 帶個訊息

- put through 使穿過；使從事；接通（電話）；為……接通電話。例如：
  Can you put me through to this number？
  你能幫我接通這個電話號碼嗎？

- arrive 是不及物動詞。到達某地，需要 + at 或 + in。
  + at 是指到達的地方範圍比較小，比如 station、cinema、park 等小地方。
  + in 是指到達的地方範圍比較大，比如 Beijing、America 等大地方。

# Chapter3  公事公辦 Business Time

## Unit 1 預約見面 Making an Appointment

### Fresh Expressions

I'd like to make an appointment with Professor Zhang, please.

我想和張教授約個時間會面。

May I call at your office sometime this week?

這週我能去辦公室拜訪你嗎？

Are you free this afternoon? I'd drop by when I'm passing.

今天下午有空嗎？我想路過時順便拜訪。

I'm sorry for the sudden notice, but I'd like to meet with you this afternoon.

恕我冒昧，今天下午我想與您會面。

What time is convenient to you?

你什麼時間方便呢？

I was wondering if we could get together sometime this afternoon.

我想今天下午我們是否可以見個面。

If you don't mind, may we put it off to the next day?

如果你不介意，我們可以延遲到第 2 天嗎？

I was wondering if you had any plans for Friday afternoon.

我想知道週五下午你是否有空。

Then I'll come over to your office at eleven o'clock Friday morning.

那我就在週五上午十一點到您的辦公室。

Not for any particular time, but he's expecting me in the office this morning.

沒有約定具體時間，但他今天上午會在辦公室等我的。

He regrets he won't be able to receive Mr. Smith tomorrow afternoon. He'll be engaged the whole afternoon.

他很抱歉明天下午不能接待史密斯先生。他整個下午都很忙。

I'm afraid not. I'm fully booked up tomorrow.

恐怕不行。我明天已排滿了。

## Interactive Dialogues

### Dialogue 1

A：Hello, is it Mr. Chang?

A：喂，請問是常先生嗎？

B：Yes.

B：是的，我是。

A：This is Victor Company. Could I call on you at a convenient time?

A：這裡是勝利公司。我能在適當時去拜訪你嗎？

B：Sure, you are welcome. It doesn't matter. But I can only afford a few minutes.

B：當然可以，歡迎你來。沒什麼關係。但我只能給你幾分鐘。

A：Oh, thank you very much. Actually it has been beyond my prediction. I heard that your company got a large order from a factory.

A：哦，非常感謝。事實上這已超出我的預期。我聽說你們公司從一家工廠得到一筆大訂單。

B：Yes, how do you know?

B：是的，你怎麼知道？

A：It's not important how do I know this. But I'm calling to make you know about our office computer. It has more features than the present office computer and could be a real time and money saver. Could you put me on your calendar for twenty minutes this weekend?

A：我是怎麼知道的並不重要。但我打電話是要讓你知道我們的辦公電腦。它比現今的辦公電腦功能多，且能真正地節省時間和金錢。這週末我能去拜訪你嗎，只要 20 分鐘？

B：Oh, I'm afraid I can't because I am going to attend a meeting this week-end.

B：哦，恐怕不行，因為週末我要參加一個會議。

A：So how about next Monday?

A：那麼下週一如何？

B：That's OK. I will be waiting for you at 9 o'clock in my office now.

B：那可以。我 9 點鐘在我的辦公室裡等你。

A：Thanks. I will be there at 9 o'clock. See you next Monday.

A：謝謝。9 點我會在那裡的。下週一再見。

B：See you later.

B：再見。

### Notes

■ call on 和 call at 的意思一樣，都是「拜訪、訪問」，但 call on 後接表示人的名詞或代詞，call at 後接表示地點或場所的詞語。例如：

I called on the Smiths yesterday.

我昨天拜訪了史密斯一家人。

I called at the Smith's yesterday.

我昨天去了史密斯家。

另外，call on 還可用作「號召」，後面往往接動詞不定式作受詞補主語。例如：

The headmaster called on the students to work harder.

校長號召學生們更努力地學習。

- at a convenient or suitable time 在適當的時候

- afford 常與 can、could、be able to 連用，意思是買的起、付得起、花得起時間、金錢、精力等。但是 afford 只表示能力，不表示意願。例如：

They did not consider whether they could afford the time or not.

他們沒有考慮是否抽得出時間。

We can't afford to pay such a price.

我們付不起這個價錢。

- beyond one's prediction 超出某人的預料

### Dialogue 2

A：Hello, I'm He Wei.

A：你好，我是何威。

B：Hello, Mr. He. Since you're so busy, I have to speak straight forward. I hope you will give me a chance to introduce our new service.

B：您好，何先生。由於您很忙，我就開門見山直說了。我希望您能給我一個機會來介紹我們的新服務。

A：Can't you mail the information to me?

A：你不能把那些訊息郵寄給我嗎？

B：Yes, I could. But everyone's situation is different. Mr. He, our service is the most convenient for you. Could you give me a few minutes?

B：是的，可以。但是每個人的情況是不同的。何先生，我們的服務可以說是專為您設計的。您能給我幾分鐘嗎？

A：Well, what do you want to talk about?

A：嗯，你想說什麼呢？

B：It's difficult to explain the service over the telephone. In 15 minutes I can show the saving and convenience you can get from the service.

B：在電話上很難解釋清楚。只要 15 分鐘我就可以向您說明我們服務的方便性和廉價性。

A：You'd just be wasting your time, I'm not interested.

A：你只是在浪費時間，我沒興趣。

B：Do you mean that you don't take an airplane or reserve a room in hotel?

B：您是說您從不搭飛機或住旅館嗎？

A：No, that's not the reason. Actually I take an airplane at least once every month. But all of this always takes me much time and energy each time.

A：不，不是這個原因。事實上我每個月至少會搭一次飛機，但是都得花費我大量的時間和精力。

B：I'm very sorry that you have such unhappy experience. But our service can just solve all these troubles. It can bring you the best convenience and satis-faction.

B：非常抱歉您有這麼不愉快的經歷。但我們的服務正可以為您解決所有麻煩。它會帶給您最大的方便和滿意。

A：Well, your sincerity drives me to grant you a choice. You may come to my office tomorrow morning.

A：嗯，你的誠摯促使我給你一個機會。你可以在明天早上到我的辦公室來。

B：Very good! That's very kind of you. Goodbye!

B：太好了！您真是太好了。再見！

### Notes

- straight forward 直截了當。例如：

  He always speaks in a direct way, and that is why we guess his writing style must be concise and straightforward.

  他說話總是直截了當，那就是為什麼我們覺得他的寫作風格一定簡明扼要。

- drives sb. to do sth. 促使某人做某事。例如：

  It drives me to save money in order to buy the car.

  為了買車，我強迫自己存錢。

- grant you a choice 給你一個機會。grant sb. sth. 賦予某人做某事的特權

## ▎Unit 2 有事拜訪 Paying a Visit

### Fresh Expressions

Will you wait a moment? I'll tell him you're here.

請稍等一下好嗎？我去通知一下。

I'm sorry to call on you without an appointment.

冒昧來訪，十分抱歉。

Would you have a seat while I give a call to Mr. Wang?

您是否可以先請坐讓我打個電話給王先生？

Please let me take you to the manager's office.

請讓我帶您去經理的辦公室。

I'll show you to his office. Please follow me.

我帶您到他的辦公室,請隨我來。

I'm sorry to have kept you waiting for a long time.

對不起,讓您久等了。

My boss should be with you in a minute.

我們老闆很快就能見您。

Thank you very much for giving us your valuable time.

我們占用了你寶貴的時間,非常感謝。

I am Mr. Gao. I have an appointment at eleven o'clock. I'm sorry, I was a little late.

我是約 11 點見面的高先生,很抱歉我稍微遲到了。

The traffic is busy. I'm afraid I'll be about thirty minutes late.

路上塞車。恐怕我會遲到約 30 分鐘。

## Interactive Dialogues

### Dialogue 1

A:Hello, I'd like to see Mr. Li, please.

A:你好,我想和李先生見面。

B:Do you have an appointment, sir?

B:先生,你有預約嗎?

A:No, I don't, but I'd like to see him just for a while.

A:沒有,但我只需與他會面一會兒。

B：May I have your name, please?

B：請告訴我你的名字，好嗎？

A：My name is David Huang.

A：我是黃大衛。

B：Can I know what you wish to see him about?

B：請問你有什麼事要見他？

A：I'd rather explain that to him directly.

A：我想直接向他說明。

B：I'm sorry, but I'm told to ask that information from every visitor.

B：抱歉，我奉命詢問每位訪客的來意。

A：I see. Well, I'm from UDN Daily and I'm wondering if he is interested in placing supplements in our newspaper.

A：原來如此。嗯，我來自《聯合日報》，我想知道他有沒有興趣在我們日報內刊登特刊。

B：I see. Just a minute, please.

B：原來如此，請稍等。

B：(use intercom) Mr. Li, Mr. David Huang of UDN Daily is here to see you. He wants to know if you are interested in placing supplements in his newspaper.

B：（用內線電話）李先生，《聯合日報》的黃大衛先生來此想見你。他想知道你有沒有興趣在他們日報內刊登特刊。

C：Well, I am quite interested. Ask him to come in, please.

C：嗯，我有興趣。請他進來見我。

B：All right, Mr. Li. (to the visitor) Mr. Huang, please go right in.

B：好的，李先生。（對客人）黃先生，請進。

A：Thank you very much.

A：非常感謝。

Notes

- be interested in 對（某人、某事物）有興趣
- supplement （書籍的）補遺；附錄；（報刊等的）增刊、副刊。例如：
  The story first appeared in the Times Literary Supplement.
  這個短篇小說第一次是發表在《泰晤士報文學副刊》上的。
- go right in 中 right 在這裡當副詞「直接地」，用來修飾動詞 go，也可以加在動詞前。right + do... 是很常見的句型，意思就是直接去做某事，潛臺詞是指比較匆忙的。

Dialogue 2

A：Have a seat, Mr. Younger. What can I do for you?

A：請坐，楊格先生。有什麼我能為你效勞的嗎？

B：I have a house in Seattle. It's about 400 sq. ft., including the house and the yard. I'm looking for somebody who will buy it in cash.

B：我在西雅圖有棟房子。大概四百平方英尺，包括房子和院子。我想找個肯花現金買它的買主。

A：How much do you want to sell it for?

A：你想賣多少錢？

B：Around half a million U.S. dollars!

B：大概 50 萬美金左右！

A：Sounds reasonable.

A：聽起來滿公道的。

B：I'd like to sell it as soon as possible for ready money.

B：我想盡快賣掉得到現款。

A：I see. Is the house under your name?

A：原來如此。房子是在你的名下嗎？

B：Yes. Here are the papers. I've also made copies of each of them. You can keep the copies.

B：是的。這裡是所有的文件。我還各影印了一份。你可以把影本留著。

A：Very well. Do you have a photo of the house with you?

A：很好。有沒有帶房子的照片來？

B：Sure. Here you are. There're six of them.

B：當然有。在這裡。一共有 6 張。

A：This one is OK, but the others.... Well, I think I'll have to send my men to take pictures of your house, pictures that are taken by a professional and are able to show the whole aspect of the house.

A：這一張不錯，但其他的……。嗯，我覺得我得派我們這裡的人去房子那裡拍照，專業攝像師拍出來的照片能夠展示房屋的整體外觀。

B：That's fine with me. What is your charge for this service? ...Er, I don't mean the pictures, I mean to be my agent.

B：沒問題。那你要分多少服務費呢？……嗯，我不是指照片，我是指代理費。

A：Well, 3% of the sale price of your house.

A：嗯，按照你出售房價的 3%算。

Notes

- in cash 用現金付款。例如：

  You can pay in cash, by credit card or with a check.

  你可以用現金支付，也可以用信用卡或支票支付。

- ready money 現款、立即付款的現金。例如：

  She had at this time ready money enough to supply all that was wanted of greater elegance to the apartments.

  此時她手裡有足夠的錢來購置一些東西，把房子布置得更加幽雅。

- aspect 方面；觀點；外觀；樣子。例如：

  The fierce aspect of the salesman frightened the customer off.

  那個店員的兇相把顧客嚇跑了。

# Unit 3 電話推銷 Promotion By Telephone

### Fresh Expressions

This offer will expire in two day.

這個特價優待 2 天內就結束了。

No other offer like this will be made in the future.

以後不會再有這樣的特價優待了。

If you are not satisfied, you may return it.

如果你不滿意，你可以退貨。

We want your 100 percent satisfaction.

我們包你百分之百的滿意。

You may take it just for a few weeks' risk-free trial.

你可以試用幾個星期。

You may order now over the phone.

你可以現在就用電話訂購。

Why not order now and take the advantage?

何不現在就訂，享受優待？

You may find out you need it in the future. Please don't hesitate to call us.

如果你以後覺得需要，請及時與我們聯絡。

Don't delay your decision. This is the best offer.

別再猶豫不決。這是最好的優待了。

## Interactive Dialogues

### Dialogue 1

A：Hello. Can I speak to the head of the household?

A：哈囉。我可以跟戶主講話嗎？

B：May I ask who's calling?

B：請問您是誰？

A：This is Jiang Ping with Children's Publishing Company. May I have your name, sir?

A：我是兒童出版公司的江平。能請教您的名字嗎，先生？

B：My name is Chen.

B：我姓陳。

A：Thank you, Mr. Chen. Do you have children?

A：謝謝你，陳先生。您有孩子嗎？

B：Yes.

B：有的。

A：Great. I think you must care for children's education.

A：太好了。我想您一定很關心孩子的教育。

B：Certainly.

B：那當然。

A：Mr. Chen, maybe you have heard about it already that Children's Pub-lishing Company has the most successful Children's English Learning Books in the market. These books will help your children a lot in learning English.

A：陳先生，可能您已聽說過兒童出版公司出版的兒少英文讀物在市場上非常成功。這些書籍對兒童學習英文有很大幫助。

B：Yes.

B：是的。

A：And we are running a special offer on the books now. I would like to tell you more about it.

A：而我們現在正在做特別優惠活動。我想為您多做介紹。

B：Oh, I'm sorry. I am kind of busy and....

B：哦，很抱歉。我現在有點忙……。

A：Mr. Chen, you can have savings of up to 50 percent, and this offer will expire in two days.

A：陳先生，您可以節省一半，且優惠期兩天後就會結束。

B：Oh, sorry, Mr. Jiang. As a matter of fact, my daughter is only eleven months old.

B：哦，抱歉，江先生。事實上我女兒才 11 個月大。

A：Oh, all right. Mr. Chen, you may find out you need it in the future, please don't hesitate to call me. Thank you for your time.

A：哦，沒關係，陳先生，如果您以後有需要，請隨時打電話給我。謝謝您的時間。

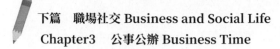
B：I appreciate your calling. Goodbye.

B：謝謝您的電話。再見。

A：Goodbye, have a nice day.

A：再見，祝您有美好的一天。

### Notes

- head of the household 戶主；一家之主

- care for 照顧；關心；喜歡；意欲。例如：

  Who will care for the house while the family is away?

  全家人都不在時，由誰照料這間房子呢？

- help…a lot in sth./do sth. 對……有很大幫助

- run a special offer 做特別優惠活動；special offer（商品等的價格）特別優惠

- kind of 常用在口語中，作副詞，表示「有點；有幾分」的意思。

- up to 多到；直到；等於；達到；適於；勝任；忙於；由……決定

- expire 滿期；屆期；（期限）終止。例如：

  My lease will expire on September 30th of this year.

  我的租約今年 9 月 30 日到期。

- as a matter of fact 事實上。例如：

  As a matter of fact, I've never been there before.

  事實上我從未到過那裡。

Dialogue 2

A：Hello, may I speak to Mr. White?

A：喂，可以讓懷特先生接電話嗎？

B：This is he speaking.

B：我就是。

A：How are you doing this evening, Mr. White?

A：懷特先生，今晚您好嗎？

B：l am fine. Who's this?

B：很好。你是哪位？

A：This is Dan, Dan Moore. I'm calling on behalf of Somy Electronics Company. Mr. White, as you know, everything now is offered with a great discount in our company.

A：我是丹，丹·摩爾。我代表索米電器公司打電話來。懷特先生，您知道，我們公司所有的東西都在大幅度打折出售。

B：Yes, l know.

B：是的，我知道。

A：Now, I'm calling to recommend you a new style of portable type recorder.

A：現在我打電話向您推薦一種新款式的便攜式錄音機。

B：Oh? Can you give me more detail, then?

B：哦？那麼你能詳細說明一下嗎？

A：Certainly, sir. This kind of recorder is completely portable and very light in weight.

A：可以，先生。這種錄音機是便攜式的，重量很輕。

B：What about the quality of the sound? Sometimes these portables sound very tiny.

B：音質怎麼樣？這種便攜式錄音機有時音量很小。

A：It's pretty good. And it'll open up a whole new world of pleasure for you and your family. You can have a free trial for two weeks, and if you are not satisfied, you may return it.

A：品質很好。它將為您和您的家庭開闢一個全新的娛樂天地。您可以免費試用兩個星期，如果不滿意，您可以退貨。

B：How much is it?

B：多少錢？

A：We'll give you a 50 percent discount. It's only 169 dollars now.

A：我們給您打五折，僅 169 美元。

B：Your offer sounds interesting.

B：聽起來滿吸引人的。

A：Yes, Mr. White. It'll save you a lot of money and virtually it's risk-free for you. We will take your order over the phone.

A：是的，懷特先生。這可以為您省很多錢，而且實際上對您而言完全沒有風險。我們可以用電話接受訂購。

B：OK, I'll take it.

B：好的，我買了。

**Notes**

- on behalf of 代表……；為了……的利益。例如：

  The lawyer spoke on behalf of his client.

  律師代表當事人說話。

- open up 開啟；開創；開闢；開放。例如：

  They decided to open up an office in the town.

  他們決定在鎮上設立一個辦事處。

- a whole new world of pleasure 一個全新的娛樂天地

- free trial 免費試用。例如：

  However, you can cancel at any time before the end of your free trial and your card will not be charged.

  不過，在免費試用期結束前，您隨時可以取消，我們不會向您的信用卡收費。

- risk-free 零風險的；沒有風險的。例如：

  Government bonds are usually referred to as risk-free bonds.

  政府債券經常被稱為無風險債券。

- take one's order 接受某人的訂單；接受某人的點菜；接受某人的安排

# Unit 4 建立合作關係 Establishing Trade Relations

## Fresh Expressions

I'm here to discuss the possibility of establishing business relations with your corporation.

我來這裡與你們商討和貴公司建立貿易關係的事宜。

I hope to conclude some business with you.

我希望能與貴公司建立貿易關係。

We are willing to enter to business relationships with your firm.

我們願意與貴公司建立業務關係。

We also hope to expand our business with you.

我們也希望與貴公司擴大貿易往來。

Our mutual understanding and cooperation will certainly result in growing business for both of us.

我們之間的相互了解與合作必將會促成今後大筆生意。

We wish to do business relations with your corporation for supply of light industrial products.

我方願與貴公司建立業務關係，以便取得輕工業產品的供貨。

We specialize in the export of German light industrial products and would like to trade with you in this line.

我們專營德國輕工業品出口業務，願與貴方就這方面開展業務往來。

We wish to express our desire to trade with you in leather shoes.

我們非常希望和你進行皮鞋的買賣生意。

We thank you for your letter offering your services and should like to discuss the possibility of expanding trade with you.

謝謝你方來函表示願意提供服務，我方願與你方就擴大貿易的可能性進行討論。

Being specialized in the export of Chinese art and craft goods, we express our desire to trade with you in this line.

我們專門出口中國工藝品，願與貴方開展這方面的業務。

We do our business on the basis of equality and mutual benefit.

我們在平等互利的基礎上做生意。

## Interactive Dialogues

### Dialogue 1

A：We invited you here today to discuss some business opportunities.

A：我們今天邀請您來就是要討論一下業務機會。

B：Great! I have a feeling that there are bright prospects for us to cooperate with in this field. I wish to do business with you.

B：太好了！我認為您我雙方在這方面合作會有良好前景。希望能和您們建立貿易關係。

A：It appears we want the same things. Concerning our financial position, credit standing and trade reputation, you may refer to Bank of Hong Kong, or to our local Chamber of Commerce or inquiry agencies.

A：您的願望和我們完全一致。關於我們的財務狀況、信用及聲譽，您們可以向香港銀行、我們的當地商會或諮詢社進行了解。

B：Thank you for your information.

B：謝謝您所提供的資訊。

A：As you know, our corporation is a state-operated one. We always trade with foreign countries on the basis of equality and mutual benefit. Establishing business relations between us will be to our mutual benefit. I have no doubt that it will bring about closer ties between us.

A：如您所知，我們公司是國營公司。我們一向是在平等互利的基礎上進行外貿交易。我們之間建立業務關係將對雙方有利。我相信業務關係的建立也會使我們之間的關係更為密切。

B：Glad to hear that. I hope this visit of mine will be the beginning of a long and friendly connection between us.

B：聽到您這麼說很高興。我希望我的這次訪問是雙方長期友好往來的開端。

## Notes

- cooperate with 合作；協作；相配合；和……合作。例如：
  We are always willing to cooperate with you and if necessary make some concessions.

我們總是願意和您合作的，如果需要還可以做些讓步。

- do business with 和……做生意，和……交往。例如：

I am only too pleased to do business with you.

我能和你做生意，太高興了。

- state-operated 國營的

- trade with 與某人交易。例如：

Specializing in the export of Chinese Cotton Piece Goods, we express our desire to trade with you in this line.

我們專門經營中國棉織品出口，願與你們進行交易。

- on the basis of 在……基礎上；以……為基礎。例如：

Is it accurate to predict the result on the basis of one secret vote?

以一次不記名投票為基礎預測結果準確嗎？

- equality and mutual benefit 平等互惠

### Dialogue 2

A：Mr. Chen, another purpose of my coming here is to inquire about possibilities of establishing long-term trade relations with your company.

A：陳先生，我此行另一個目的是想探詢與貴公司建立長期業務關係的可能性。

B：Your desire to establish long-term business relations with us coincides with ours, but....

B：您方想與我方建立長期業務關係的願望與我方是一致的，但是……。

A：Concerning our financial position, credit standing and trade reputation, you may refer to New York Branch, the Bank of Taiwan, or to our local chamber of commerce.

A：關於我們的財務狀況、信用、聲譽，可向臺灣銀行紐約分行或當地商會進行了解。

B：Thank you for your information. I think that establishing business relations between us will be benefit to both of us.

B：感謝您方提供的訊息。我想我們之間建立業務關係，將有益於我們雙方。

A：This is my first visit to your company. I'd appreciate your kind consideration in the coming negotiations.

A：這是我初次拜訪貴公司。未來洽談中請您多加關照。

B：We are very happy to be of help. I can assure you of our close cooperation.

B：我們十分樂意協助。我能保證全力合作。

A：One can always expect a fair deal when trading with Taiwan. Everyone speaks highly of your commercial integrity.

A：跟臺灣人做買賣，人們總會得到公平交易。大家都高度讚揚您們的商業信譽。

B：One of our principles is to see to it that contracts are honored and commercial integrity maintained.

B：我們的一條原則是務必要重合約、守信用。

A：If your prices are reasonable, I'll give you a special inquiry.

A：如果您方價格合理，我方將立即進行專門詢價。

B：Then, we'll try to make an offer as soon as possible. I hope a lot of business will be put through between us.

B：我們將盡快報價。我們希望我們之間能做成許多生意。

Notes

- establish long-term business relations 建立長期業務關係
- be of help 有幫助；有用
- assure sb. of sth. 使某人確信某事；使某人對某事放心；委託某人某事
- speak highly of 讚賞某人；對某人有高度評價。例如：

  We speak highly of their work and extend our deep gratitude to them.

  對於他們的工作，我們給予高度的評價並致以深深的謝意。

- commercial integrity 商業信譽。例如：

  No wonder everyone speak highly of your commercial integrity.

  難怪大家都極為推崇你們的商業信譽。

- see to 注意；負責；照料；修理；修補；診治；務必做到。例如：

  You ought to have your eyes seen to by a doctor.

  你應該請醫生醫治眼睛。

- make an offer 出價；發價

# Unit 5 銷售談判 Negotiation by Salesperson

## Fresh Expressions

Product is doing very well in foreign countries.

這種產品在國外很暢銷。

Our product is competitive in the international market.

我們的產品在國際市場上具有競爭力。

We are supplying a full range of silk products to East Asia.

我們正向東亞各國輸出全系列的絲織品。

The appearance of a package that catches the eye will certainly be of must help in promotion the sales.

引人注目的外觀包裝肯定大大有助於促銷。

These products are of the best quality and excellently made too.

這些產品品質上乘，而且製造精細。

We always keep an eye on customers' preference and make our products according to what our customers need, want and like.

我們總是密切注意客戶的喜好，且根據客戶需求和愛好生產產品。

We are always willing to cooperate with you and if necessary make some concessions.

我們總是願意合作的，如果需要還可以做些讓步。

I hope you can have these goods delivered before the end of October.

我希望你方能在 10 月底前交貨。

I'm glad our negotiation has come to a successful conclusion.

我很高興這次洽談圓滿成功。

I hope this will lead to further business between us.

我希望這次交易將讓我們之間的貿易得到進一步發展。

## Interactive Dialogues

### Dialogue 1

A：Good morning, Mr. Brown. Glad to meet you.

A：早安，布朗先生。很高興見到您。

B：Good morning, Ms. Han. It's very nice to see you in person. Let me introduce my colleagues to you. This is my manager, Mr. Thomas.

B：早安，韓女士。很高興見到您本人。讓我向您介紹一下我的同

事，這是我的上司，托馬斯先生。

A：How do you do? Mr. Thomas.

A：您好，托馬斯先生。

C：How do you do? Ms. Han.

C：您好，韓女士。

A：…And this is Mr. Wang. He is in charge of sales department.

A：……這位是王先生。銷售部主管。

B：Nice to meet you, Mr. Wang.

B：很高興見到您，王先生。

D：Nice to meet you, Mr. Brown.

D：很高興見到您，布朗先生。

A：I hope through your visit we can settle the price for our Chinaware, and conclude the business before long.

A：我希望透過您們這次來訪能把我們這批瓷器的價格定下來，很快結束這筆生意。

B：I think so, Ms. Han. We came here to talk to you about our requirements of HX Series Chinaware. Can you show us your price-list and catalogues?

B：我也是這麼想的，韓女士。我們這次來就是要和您們談我們對 HX 系列瓷器的需求。能讓我們看看價格表和商品目錄嗎？

A：We've specially made out a price-list which covers those items most popular on your market. Here you are.

A：我們專門製作了價格表，上面包括您方市場上最受歡迎的產品。給您。

B：Oh, it's very considerate of you. If you'll excuse me, I'll go over your price-list right now.

B：哦，您們考慮的真周全。如果您不介意的話，我想現在就瀏覽一下。

A：Take your time, Mr. Brown.

A：不著急，您慢慢看，布朗先生。

B：Oh, Mr. Wang. After going over your price-list and catalogues, we are interested in Art No. HX1115 and HX 1128, but we found that your price are too high than those offered by other suppliers. It would be impossible for us to push any sales at such high prices.

B：哦，王先生。看完您們的價格表和商品目錄後，我們對型號為 HX1115 和 HX 1128 的藝術品很感興趣，但是我們發現您們的價格比其他 供應商要高出很多。以這麼高的價格我們無法銷售出去。

D：I'm sorry to hear that. You must know that the cost of production has risen a great deal in recent years while our prices of Chinaware basically remain unchanged. To be frank, our commodities have always come up to our export standard and the packages are excellent designed and printed. So our products are moderately priced.

D：聽到這個很遺憾。但是您肯定知道近幾年生產成本大幅上升，而 我們產品的價格基本上維持沒變。坦率地講，我們的商品一直都能達到出 口標準，包裝都是精心設計和印製的。所以我們的產品定價適當。

B：I'm afraid I can't agree with you in this respect. I know that your products are attractive in design, but I wish to point out that your offers are higher than some of the quotations I've received from your competitors in other countries. So, your price is not competitive in this market.

B：在這一點上我恐怕無法同意。我知道您們的產品設計很吸引人， 但是我想指出您們的報價比您們在其他國家的競爭對手所提報的價格還 高。所以您們的價格在市場上並沒有競爭力。

D：Mr. Brown. As you may know, our products which are of high quality have found a good market in many countries. So you must take quality into consideration, too.

D：布朗先生。您可能知道，我們高品質的產品在許多國家都有很好的市場。所以您要把品質因素也考慮進去。

B：I agree with what you say, but the price difference should not be so big. If you want to get the order, you'll have to lower the price. That's reasonable, isn't it?

B：我同意您所說的，但是價格差距也不應該這麼大。如果您想要拿到這筆訂單，您不得不考慮降價。那很合理，不是嗎？

D：Well, in order to help you develop business in this line, we may consider making some concessions in your price, but never to that extent.

D：嗯，為了幫助您方發展業務，我們可以考慮在價格上做些讓步，但是絕對無法太大程度。

B：If you are prepared to cut down your price by 8%, we might come to terms.

B：如果您準備把您們的價格降下 8%，我們就能達成協議。

D：8%? I'm afraid you are asking too much. Actually, we have never given such lower price. For friendship's sake, we may exceptionally consider reducing the price by 5%. This is the highest reduction we can afford.

D：8% 嗎？恐怕您殺得太多了。事實上，我們從未給過那麼低的價格。出於友誼的考慮，我破例考慮降價 5%。這是我們能給的最優惠的價格了。

B：You certainly have a way of talking me into it. But I wonder if when we place a larger order, you'll farther reduce your prices. I want to order one container of HX1115 and 438 sets of HX1128.

B：您真有辦法，把我說服了。但是我想知道如果到時候我們訂單量更大，您能不能再進一步降價。我想訂一集裝箱型號為 HX1115 和 438 套型號 HX1128 產品。

D：Mr. Brown, I can assure you that our price is most favorable. We are sorry to say that we can't bring our price down a still lower level.

D：布朗先生，我可以向您保證我們的價格是最優惠的了。而且很抱歉，我們不能再把價格往下降了。

B：OK, I accept.

B：好，我接受。

**Notes**

- in person 親自。例如：

  He will be present at the meeting in person.

  他將親自參加會議。

- settle the price 定價格

- before long 等於 soon。before long 是介詞詞組，在句中作時間副詞，意為「不久之後；立刻」，常用於未來時態。例如：

  I hope we'll meet again before long.

  我希望不久我們再見面。

  long before 等於 long long ago，有兩種用法：

  - 老早、早就（單獨使用，表示比過去某時更早的時間）。例如：

    She had left long before.

    她老早就離開了。

    That had happened long before.

    那事老早就發生了。

註：long ago 表示「很久以前」，指的是從現在算起的很久以前，通常與一般過去式連用。例如：

I met him long ago.

我很久以前就認識他了。

- 在……的很久以前；在還沒有……的很久以前。例如：

She had left long before his return (he returned).

在他回來的很久以前她就走了。

He had worked in the factory long before he got married.

在他還沒有結婚的很久以前他就在這家工廠工作了。

註：此時的主句謂語通常用過去完成式，但有時也可用一般過去式（因為 before 已表現了動作的先後關係）。例如：

This happened long before you were born.

這事在你還沒出生以前很久就發生了。

■ go over 仔細檢查；查看。例如：

We should like to go over the house before deciding whether we want to buy it.

我們應先仔細查看這間房子，然後再決定是否要買。

■ at such high prices 以這麼高的價格

■ a great deal 大量的；非常。例如：

A great deal of work awaits me.

許多工作等著我去做。

He likes to swim a good deal.

他非常喜歡游泳。

■ take into consideration 考慮到；顧及；把……考慮進去。例如：

They are highly competitive when you take quality into consideration.

當你考慮到品質時，你會發現它們是很具有競爭力的。

- make a concession 做出讓步；服從

- to that extent 達到那樣的程度

- cut down 削減；降低。例如：

  He tried to cut down on smoking but failed.

  他試圖少抽菸，但沒成功。

- come to terms 達成協議。例如：

  That couple have come to terms on their divorce.

  那對夫妻已對他們的離婚達成協議。

- for friendship's sake 出於友誼的考慮。for one's sake = for the sake of，意為「由於……緣故」、「為了……利益」。

- talk sb. into doing sth. 勸說某人做某事

Dialogue 2

A：Now let's talk about the terms of payment. Would you accept D/P? I hope it will be acceptable to you.

A：現在我們來談論一下付款方式。你們同意付款交單的方式嗎？我希望你們能接受。

B：The terms of payment we usually adopt are sight L/C.

B：我們一直採用的付款方式都是即期信用狀。

A：But I think it would be beneficial to both of us to adopt more flexible payment terms such as D/P term.

A：但我想採取更靈活的付款方式對我們雙方都是有益的，例如付款交單。

B：Payment by L/C is our usual practice of doing business with all customers for such commodities. I'm sorry we can't accept D/P terms.

229

B：對於這種商品，信用狀是我們與客戶做生意時慣用的付款方式。抱歉我們不能接受付款交單。

A：As for regular orders in future, couldn't you agree to D/P?

A：考慮將來的經常性訂貨，你們能否同意採用付款交單呢？

B：Sure. After several smooth transactions, we can try D/P terms.

B：當然。經過幾輪順利的交易後，我們可以嘗試付款交單的方式。

A：Well, as for shipment, the soon the better.

A：嗯，至於裝船，我想越快越好。

B：Yes, shipment is to be made in April, not allowing partial shipment.

B：沒問題，裝船會在四月份，不允許分批裝運。

A：OK, I see. How about packing the goods?

A：好，我明白。產品如何包裝？

B：We'll pack HX1115 in carton of one set each, HX1128 in cases of one set each, two cases to a carton.

B：我們會把 HX1115 型號的每套裝一個紙箱，HX1128 每套裝入一個小包裝盒，然後兩個小盒裝入一個紙箱。

A：I suggest the goods packed in cardboard boxes, it's more attractive than cartons. Do you think so?

A：我建議商品用紙板箱包裝，看起來比紙箱更有吸引力。你不這麼認為嗎？

B：Well, I hope the packing will be attractive, too.

B：當然，我也希望包裝能更吸引人。

A：For transaction concluded on CIF basis, insurance is to be covered by the sellers for 110% of invoice value against WPA, Clash & Breakage and War Risk.

A：按 CIF 價成交的話，保險由賣方照發票金額的 110%投保水漬險、碰損破碎險和戰爭險。

B：This term less these goods should damage in transit. I agree with it.

B：這險種應該可以減少這些貨物在運輸過程中的損壞。我同意。

A：I'm glad we have brought this transaction to a successful conclusion and hope this will be the beginning of other business in the future. Let's confirm these items we concluded at the moment.

A：我很高興我們已成功地達成了交易，希望這將成為我們今後其他貿易的開端。我們來核實一下剛剛敲定的事項吧！

B：Yes, we concluded as follows: 532 sets of HX1115 at the price of USD 23.5 per set to be packed in cardboard boxes of one set each and to be shipped CIF5 Toronto. 438 sets of HX1128 at the price of USD 14.5 per set to be packed in case of one set each, two cases to a cardboard box and to be shipped CIF5 Toronto.

B：好的，我們已經談好了以下內容：532 套型號為 HX1115，價格為每套 23.5 美元，紙板箱包裝，每套裝一箱，CIF 運至多倫多含佣金 5%。438 套型號 HX1128，價格為每套 14.5 美元，每套裝入一個小包裝盒，兩小盒裝人一個紙板箱，CIF 運至多倫多含佣金 5%。

A：All right. By the way, when can I expect to sign the S/C?

A：好了。順便問一下，什麼時候能簽合約？

B：Mr. Brown, would it be convenient for you to come again tomorrow morning? I'll get the S/C ready tomorrow for your signature.

B：布朗先生，你明天上午過來方便嗎？我會把合約準備好等你簽字。

A：OK.

A：好的。

B：See you and thanks for coming, Mr. Brown.

B：再見，感謝你的到來，布朗先生。

### Notes

- D/P（Documents against Payment）是付款交單，為銀行託收的一種，賣方將單據交給銀行，透過當地託收行，買方付款贖單提貨。在此過程中銀行不承擔任何風險責任。

- L/C（Letter of Credit）是信用狀，這是在國際貿易中普遍運用的一種交易方式，它的風險較低，由銀行來作為仲介，是一種銀行信用，但交易雙方向銀行繳納的費用很高，現在在交易中也出現了信用狀詐欺的問題，所以使用時也應謹慎選擇。

- CIF（Cost, Insurance and Freight）是包括保險費的到港價，即賣方不僅要承擔到達收貨人港口前的海運費、陸運費，還要承擔保險費。

- WPA 即水漬險，意為單獨海損賠償，是海洋運輸保險的主要險別之一，它高於平安險（FPA），但低於一切險（All Of Risks）。

- S/C 是 sales contract 的縮寫，意思就是銷售合約。

## Unit 6 砍價折扣交易 Mark-down and Discount

### Fresh Expressions

I heard other stores were having great mark-downs on this item.

聽說別家的這個東西在大降價。

If the price is higher than that, we'd rather call the whole deal off.

如果價格比那高，我們情願放棄這筆交易。

I'm afraid I could not agree with you for such a big discount.

恐怕我不能同意給你這麼大的折扣。

In this way, it won't leave us anything.

這樣的話，我方就無利可圖了。

Considering the long-standing business relationship between us, we shall grant you special discount of 12%.

考慮我們之間長期的業務關係，我們將給你們 12%的特別折扣。

But 12% discount is not enough for such a big order.

但對這麼大的訂單來說，12%的折扣是不夠的。

Only for very special customers do we allow them a rate of 12% discount.

只有對非常特殊的客戶，我們才給 12%的折扣。

Besides, the price of this product is tending up.

另外，這種產品的價格正在上漲。

Anyhow, let's meet each other half-way, how about 18%?

不管怎樣，我們相互讓步，18%的折扣怎麼樣？

All right, I agree to give you 18% discount provided you order 150,000 sets.

好，我同意給 18%的折扣，但你得訂購 150,000 臺才行。

## Interactive Dialogues

### Dialogue 1

A：Welcome to our company. My name is Jeff Kim. I'm in charge of the export department. Let me give you my business card.

A：歡迎到我們公司來。我叫金傑夫，負責出口部。這是我的名片。

B：I'll give you mine too.

B：也給你我的名片。

A：How was your flight?

A：你的航行順利嗎？

B：Not bad, but I'm little tired.

B：還可以，不過我有點累。

A：Here's your schedule. After this meeting, we will visit the factory and have another meeting with the production manager. And you'll be having dinner with our director.

A：這是你的行程安排。開完會後，我們去參觀工廠，再跟生產部經理開個會。晚上你將和我們主任共進晚餐。

B：Could you arrange a meeting with your boss?

B：你能安排我跟你們老闆開個會嗎？

A：Of course, I've arranged it at 10 o'clock tomorrow morning.

A：當然可以，我會安排在明天早上 10 點。

B：Well, shall we get down to business?

B：嗯，那我們開始談正事吧？

A：Sure, did you receive the sample we sent last week?

A：當然好，你有沒有收到我們上週寄給你的樣品？

B：Yes, we finished the evaluation of it. If the price is acceptable we would like to order now.

B：收到了，我們已進行評估。如果價格合適，我們現在就想訂貨。

A：I'm very glad to hear that.

A：聽到這個我很高興。

B：What's your best price for that item?

B：這種貨你們最低價是多少？

A：The unit price is $12.50.

A：單價是 12.50 美元。

B：I think the price is a little high, can't you reduce it?

B：我覺得這個價格貴了點，你能不能減一點？

A：I'm afraid we can't. $12.50 is our rock bottom price. If you purchase more than 10,000 units we can reduce it to $12.00.

A：恐怕不行。12.50 美元是我們的最低價。如果你訂貨超過 10,000 件，我們可以減到 12.00 美元。

B：Well, I'll accept the price and place an initial order of 10,000 units.

B：可以，我接受這個價格，第一批訂 10,000 件。

A：Very good. It's been a pleasure to do business with you, Mr. Smith.

A：太好了。史密斯先生，跟你做生意真是我的榮幸。

B：The pleasure is ours. Can you deliver the goods by March 31?

B：是我們的榮幸才對。你們可以在 3 月 31 號前發貨嗎？

A：Of course.

A：當然可以。

## Notes

- have dinner with sb. 與某人共進晚餐

- get down to business 開始做正事；辦正經事。例如：

  After some pleasant talk, we got down to business.

  寒暄談笑後，我們開始做正事。

- rock bottom price 最低價。例如：

  This is the rock bottom price and any further reduction is out of the question.

  這是最低價格，無法進一步降價。

Dialogue 2

A：Mr. He, I've considered the offer you made me yesterday. I must point out that your price is much higher than other quotations we've received.

A：何先生，我已經考慮過您昨天給我的報價。我必須指出您方的價格比我們收到的其他報價高多了。

B：Well, it may appear a little higher, but the quality of our products is much better than that of other suppliers. You must take this into consideration.

B：嗯，價格可能有點高，不過我們的產品品質也比其他供貨商好。這點您必須得考慮到。

A：I agree with you on this point. Otherwise, we would simply stop doing business with you. This time I intend to place a large order but business is almost impossible unless you give me a discount.

A：我同意您的這個觀點。不過，我們不能跟您們做生意。這次我想訂一大批貨，可是如果您們不給我折扣的話，這筆生意幾乎不可能做成。

B：If so, we'll certainly give you a discount. But how large is the order you intend to place with us?

B：如果是這樣，我方肯定會給您折扣。但您打算跟我們下的訂單有多大呢？

A：100,000 sets with a discount rate of 25%.

A：訂購 100,000 臺，折扣 25%。

B：I am afraid I could not agree with you for such a big discount. In this way, it won't leave us anything. Our maximum is 12%.

B：恐怕我不能同意給您這麼大的折扣。這樣的話，我方就無利可圖了。我方最大的折扣為 12%。

A：Oh, Mr. He, you see, with such a large order on hand, you needn't worry any more. You don't have to take in new orders. Think it over. We are old friends.

A：哦，何先生，您看，手裡有這麼大的訂單，您就無需再擔心了。您們不必再接受新訂單了。好好考慮一下。我們是老朋友了。

B：Considering the long-standing business relationship between us we shall grant you special discount of 12%. As you know, we do business on the basis of equality and mutual benefit.

B：考慮到我們之間的長期貿易關係，我們將給您們12％的特別折扣。如您所知，我們是在平等互惠的基礎上做生意的。

A：Yes, I also hope we do business on mutually beneficial basis. But 12% discount is not enough for such a big order.

A：是的，我也希望我們在互利的基礎上做生意。但是對於這麼大的訂單，12％的折扣是不夠的。

B：Only for very special customers do we allow them a rate of 12% discount. Besides, the price of this product is tending up. There is a heavy demand for it.

B：只有對非常特殊的客戶，我們才給12％的折扣。此外，這種產品的價格正在上漲。這種產品的需求量很大。

A：Yes, I know the present tendency. Anyhow, let's meet each other half-way, how about 18%?

A：是的，我明白目前的趨勢。好，我們互相讓步，18%怎麼樣？

B：You are a real businessman! All right, I agree to give you 18% discount provided you order 150,000 sets.

　　B：您真是個精明的生意人！好，我同意給您 18％的折扣，但您得訂購 150,000 臺才行。

　　A：OK. I accept.

　　A：好，我接受。

**Notes**

- place an order 下（放）訂單；訂貨。例如：

　　If you come down to the old price, we can place an order of a large quantity.

　　貴方若能降到老價格，我們就向您大量訂貨。

- on hand 在手頭；在近處。例如：

　　I always like to keep a certain amount of money on hand.

　　我總喜歡在手頭備好一筆錢。

- take in 接受；吸收；接納；理解；領會；欺騙；包括

- Think it over. 好好想想；好好考慮一下吧；仔細考慮一下

- a heavy demand 需求量很大

# Chapter4
## 社交門道 Social Courtesy

## ▌Unit 1 贈送禮物 Sending Gifts

### Fresh Expressions

Here's a little token of my affection.

送你這件小禮物作為友誼的表示。

Please accept this little gift as a souvenir.

請留下這個小小禮物作為紀念。

That's so nice of you. Shall I open it?

你人太好了。我能打開看看嗎？

I sent her a gift as a token of my congratulation.

我寄給她一個禮物表示祝賀。

I send you this gift as a mark of esteem.

我送你這件禮物以表敬意。

To apologize for leaving so early, I brought you a little gift.

為了表示我提早離開的歉意，我帶了一件小禮物給你。

I present the gift as a token of our appreciation for what you've done for us.

我用這個禮物作為象徵，對你為我們所做的一切表示感激。

Please accept this gift in token of our affection for you.

請接受這份禮物，這是我們微薄的情意。

If you are going to collect some money for a gift for her, you can count me in.

假如你們要出錢給她當禮物，可以算我一份。

## Interactive Dialogues

### Dialogue 1

A：Jessica is going back to America next week. I've been thinking a lot about what to give her as a parting gift, but I still have no clue.

A：潔西卡下週就要回美國了。我一直在想該選什麼東西作為分別的禮物，但是還沒有頭緒。

B：Is that the girl you spent almost every weekend with?

B：是那個幾乎每週都和你在一起的女孩嗎？

A：Yeah, that's her. We had a lot of wonderful times together. She is really a special friend, and I want to get her something meaningful.

A：是的，就是她。我們在一起有過很多快樂的時光。她是一個很特別的朋友，我想送給她一件有意義的禮物。

B：I am not good at picking gifts. Maybe you can ask if there's anything she needs to make it easier?

B：我也不太會挑禮物。要不你先問問她想要什麼，這樣就能容易點？

A：I don't think so. That way it would lose all the charm. I want it to be a surprise. I want to show her that I care about her and I hope our friendship will last.

A：我不這麼想。那樣就沒意思了。我想給她一個驚喜。我想讓她知道我很珍惜她，希望我們的友誼能長存。

B：Yeah, that's nice.

B：嗯，這樣不錯。

A：Hmm, I think I've got an idea. Maybe I can get her an ever-green plant to take back home.

A：嗯，我有想法了。或許我可以送她一盆長青植物讓她帶回家。

B：A plant? That's creative. I'm sure every time she waters it she'll think of you. But there is a problem. Do you think it'll be able to go through the customs?

B：一盆植物？滿有創意的。我相信她澆水時總能想起你。但是有一個問題。你覺得植物能過海關嗎？

A：I hope so. I'll make sure to get a small one so she can put it into her suitcase. I hope it won't cause her trouble at the border.

A：希望如此。我會選個小的，這樣她就能放在箱子裡面。我不想過海關時讓她惹麻煩。

B：I don't know. I think the idea of a plant going across borders with a friend is really exciting but maybe seeds would be safer. You don't want to get her in trouble.

B：我不清楚。我覺得送朋友植物，帶著它穿越國界，這想法本身就讓人特別興奮。但是可能種子會更安全一點。畢竟你不想讓她有麻煩。

## Notes

- have no clue 無頭緒；無線索。例如：
  We have no clue as to where she went after she left home.
  我們對她離家後去往何處毫無線索。
- lose all the charm 沒什麼意思；失去魅力
- an ever-green plant 一盆長青的植物
- go through the customs 過海關
- cause trouble 惹麻煩；招致麻煩；製造麻煩。例如：

He's picking on Peter, and you know Peter's the last man in the world to cause trouble.

他老是跟彼得過不去，而你知道彼得是最安分守己的人。

- go across borders 穿越國界；go across 穿過。例如：

We can go across the frozen river.

我們可以橫渡這凍結了的河。

- get sb. in trouble 使某人陷入困境；給某人帶來麻煩

### Dialogue 2

A：This is the first time I've been in Taiwan, and everything here fascinated me. But there is something I can never figure out!

A：這是我第一次來臺灣，這裡的一切都吸引我。但有件事我總是無法理解！

B：What's wrong? Did anything puzzle you, speak it up and see if I can help you out.

B：怎麼了？有什麼不明白的，說出來看看我能不能幫你。

A：Good! You turn up so timely! I am just expecting some good explanation. You know the other day one of my Taiwan friends was celebrating his birthday so I asked him what he would like for a birthday present. Do you know what he said? "No, no! Don't give me anything. Don't be polite!" Can you believe it?

A：太好了！你簡直出現得太及時了！我正想找到好的解釋。有一天我的一個臺灣朋友過生日，我問他想要什麼禮物。你知道他說什麼嗎？他說：「不，不！什麼都別送。別客氣。」你能相信嗎？

B：Actually, I can well believe it. It's a Taiwan way of expressing his being humble and reserved. But most often the speaker doesn't really mean refusal unless he firmly insists. Taiwan people don't easily accept the given things only when he has contributed to the giver or there is an intimacy. And they don't want their friends "pofei" which means to spend money.

B：事實上，我相信。因為這只是臺灣式的客氣和矜持。通常情況下說話者並不是真的表示拒絕，除非他堅決不要。臺灣人只有在幫過忙或關係親密的朋友之間才接受饋贈。他們不想讓朋友「破費」── 花錢。

A：What did he mean by refusing to accept a present from me then?

A：那他拒絕接受我的禮物是什麼意思？

B：I don't think he was actually refusing to accept a present from you. It was just his way of being "polite." He didn't mean to be rude and certainly he didn't mean to offend you.

B：我認為他並不是真的拒絕接受你的禮物。只是他「客氣」的一種方式。他並不是有意無禮，當然，他並非有意要冒犯你。

A：Well, how do you like that? And what was I supposed to do or say in such a situation?

A：哦，那你是怎麼看的？那碰到這種情況我該怎麼說或怎麼做呢？

B：You should first understand that Taiwan people are not straightforward in some situation. In such a situation I suggest you just insist, and if your friend is an elderly gentleman, you probably have to insist several times, but even then I doubt if he will ever give you a direct answer. Or you can buy him a gift directly without asking him. I think he will be satisfied with whatever you buy him. Actually what counts is your good intention.

B：首先要明白臺灣人在有些情況下並不是很直接的。在這種情況下我建議你必須一再堅持，如果對方是位老先生，你還得再多堅持幾次，但

243

即便如此我想他可能還是不會給你直接的回覆。或你可以直接買好禮物而不必問他。朋友們一定會高興的，畢竟重要的是你的一份心意。

A：So you mean buying a gift is a good choice than not, right?

A：所以你的意思是買禮物比不買還好，對嗎？

B：I think so.

B：是的。

A：Thank you.

A：謝謝你。

**Notes**

■ fascinate 迷住；使神魂顛倒；強烈地吸引。例如：

The child was fascinated with his new toy.

那孩子對他的新玩具著了迷。

■ figure out 計算出；估計；理解。例如：

I can't figure him out.

我看不透他。

■ help sb. out 意思是「幫助解決難題（幫助擺脫困境；幫助完成；救出）」。例如：

He refused to accept help out of a false sense of pride.

他由於死要面子而不肯接受幫助。

■ turn up 在這句話裡的意思是「出現；露面」。此時 turn up 相當於 show up、appear、come out。例如：

We invited her to dinner but she didn't even bother to turn up.

我們請她吃飯她都不露面。

- humble 謙遜的；謙恭的；（身分、地位等）低下的；卑微的。例如：

  Many famous people are surprisingly humble.

  許多知名人士都出奇地謙遜。

  He is of humble birth.

  他出身卑微。

- intimacy 熟悉；親密；親近。例如：

  An intimacy grew up between us.

  我們之間的關係親密起來了。

- straight forward 直率的；正直的；老實的；坦率的。例如：

  I must insist on your giving me a straightforward answer.

  我一定要你給我一個直截了當的回答。

- what counts is... 重要的是……

# Unit 2 請客吃飯 My Treat

## Fresh Expressions

We're getting up a dinner party to you and it will be held at the Garden Hotel at eight this evening.

我們今晚 8 點鐘在花園酒店為你接風洗塵。

Since it is hot today, I'm sure a beer after work will taste wonderful.

既然天氣這麼熱，我覺得工作結束後喝一杯啤酒會特別爽快。

Please yourself at home.

請隨便。（請不要拘束。）

Please have a seat.

請入席。

On behalf of our company, I would like to say how delighted we are to receive you here.

我代表我們公司，對在這裡接待你們表示十分高興。

Thank you very much for preparing such a splendid dinner especially for us.

十分感謝專門為我們準備的豐盛宴席。

Let's hope for good cooperation between us.

希望我們能合作愉快。

May I propose a toast to the expansion of trade between Taiwan and the United States?

為臺美貿易的發展乾杯。

Thank you very much for your hospitality.

非常感謝你的盛情招待。

Thank you very much for giving us your valuable time.

我們占用了你寶貴的時間，非常感謝。

## Interactive Dialogues

### Dialogue 1

A：Mr. Carter, I'm Alice, secretary of Mr. Huang. I'm coming to fetch you. Mr. Huang is waiting for you at Huangdu Great Hotel. This way please.

A：卡特先生，我是黃先生的祕書愛麗絲。我來接您。黃先生正在皇都大飯店等您。請這邊走。

B：Thank you, Miss. Alice.

B：謝謝，愛麗絲小姐。

C：Good evening, Mr. Carter. I'm so glad you were able to come. Now dinner's ready. Let's go over to the dinner table. Would you sit here on my right,

Mr. Carter?

C：晚安，卡特先生。很高興您來能。飯菜都準備好了。我們去餐桌就坐吧！卡特先生，您坐在我右邊好嗎？

B：Glad to meet you again, Mr. Huang. You're so kind.... Oh, it's a real Chinese meal, using chopsticks.

B：很高興再次見到您，黃先生。您太客氣了……。哦，這是一頓真正的中餐，要用筷子。

C：Yes. Hope you like it. Do you need beer or wine?

C：是的。希望您能喜歡。您要啤酒還是白酒？

B：Beer, please. Oh, there are so many dishes.

B：啤酒就好。哇，這麼多菜。

C：These are cold dishes. Cold dishes are starters at a Chinese dinner. Main courses and soup come later.... Try some of this, please.

C：這是冷盤。吃中餐時先上冷盤。主菜和湯隨後上……。請嚐嚐這道菜。

B：That's delicious. Can you tell me what this is?

B：真好吃。您能告訴我這道菜叫什麼嗎？

C：Yes, it's roast duck, a specialty of this region. You have it hot and it's very nice.

C：可以，這是烤鴨，本地特色菜。您趁熱吃，味道很好。

B：I see. And what's that?

B：我知道了。那是什麼菜？

C：Well, that's something rather special. It's called fried spare ribs with sweet and sour sauce.

C：哦，那道菜很有特色。叫糖醋排骨。

B：It smells very nice. I'd like to have some more. It's delicious.

B：聞起來很香。我想再來點。真好吃。

C：I'm glad you like them.... Let's drink to our friendship.

C：很高興您喜歡這些菜……。來為我們的友誼乾一杯吧！

B：I agree. And I hope we can broaden the cooperative fields.

B：我同意。同時我希望能擴大我們合作的領域。

### Notes

■ Well, that's something rather special. 中「something」在此處表示「很不錯的東西」，「rather」在句中的意思是「相當」。

■ drink to 意為「為……乾杯，為……祝福」，這是一個固定搭配，類似於 dance to 是「跟著音樂跳舞」。

■ spare rib 英文解釋為 a cut of pork ribs with much of the meat trimmed off，意為「（豬的）帶肉肋骨」。rib 當動詞時，意為「裝肋於；用肋狀物支撐（或圍住）」；當名詞時，意為「肋骨」。trim off 意為「把……修剪掉」。

■ broaden the cooperative fields 擴大合作的領域

### Dialogue 2

A：This is a nice-looking place, Mr. Green, nice atmosphere, pleasant decor, and polite service.

A：格林先生，這是個很雅緻的地方，氣氛好、裝潢討好、服務快又有禮。

B：They also have a wide variety of dishes from different European and North American styles.

B：而且這餐廳供應很多種菜色，有歐洲及美式口味的。

A：Seems they've chosen their location wisely as well; right downtown in the business and retail district.

A：這家餐廳的地點似乎也選得極佳，正位於市中心的商業與零售區。

B：Indeed. They've sold franchise operations all across the island. I've also heard they intend to expand across Asia and to the west coast of the US.

B：沒錯。他們亦在全島廣建加盟店。我還聽說他們有意在亞洲拓展事業，還有美國西岸各地。

C：They've certainly got the money to do it too, judging from customer turnover.

C：從顧客的人數來看，他們絕對有足夠的資金那麼做。

B：You know, their capital turnover is unbelievable. They cater to the entertainment needs of all the local mom-and-pop international businesses.

B：您知道，資本週轉相當驚人。他們符合許多小型國際化公司招待國外客戶的需求。

A：Sounds like they've discovered a real gold-mine here.

A：似乎他們在此發掘到金礦了。

D：May I take your orders now?

D：現在要點菜了嗎？

B：Would you like to order first, Ms. Joanna?

B：喬安娜女士，您要不要先點？

C：Can we rely on your knowledge of wines, Ms. Joanna?

C：喬安娜女士，我們可以信賴您的品酒知識吧？

A：Well, I'm not an expert, but I do like a good Rhine wine once in a while.

A：嗯，我可不是這方面的專家，但有時我喜歡來一杯葡萄酒。

C：I'm sure we'll all be really satisfied.

C：我想我們都會非常滿意的。

A：I know both of you ordered dishes with red meat, and the rule is usually red wine with red meat, white with white. But that rule is breaking down; at least in North America.

A：我知道您們兩位點了紅肉的主菜，一般規則是紅肉配紅酒、白肉配白酒。但這種舊俗已漸漸沒人遵守了，至少在美加當地是如此。

C：North Americans seem to be pretty laid-back about most rules of etiquette.

C：美加人士似乎對許多禮儀上的規定很不在意。

A：Uh-huh. I know I'm your guest here in Taiwan, gentlemen, but I would really like to pay for the meal if you don't mind, since you've been so good to me.

A：哦。先生們，我知道我是您們在臺灣的客人，但如果兩位不介意，我希望這一頓由我請客，因為您們對我太照顧了。

B：I'm afraid I've pulled a fast one on you, Ms. Joanna. I always prepay at this restaurant.

B：喬安娜女士，我想我恐怕把您騙倒了。在這家餐廳我每次都先付錢。

**Notes**

- judging from 由……看來；根據……。根據語法規則，主要子句與分詞子句的主詞必需一致，才能將分詞子句之主詞省略。但「judging from」用作獨立結構，即不用考慮從句和主句邏輯關係的一致性，故

「judging from」該子句所省略之主詞,與後接之主要子句之主詞雖不一致,仍為正確用法。例如:

Judging from his sales performance, he will definitely be promoted to department manager.

從他的業績來看,他一定會升任部門經理。

- cater to 迎合;為……服務。例如:

Our literature and art ought to cater to popular taste.

我們的文藝應該為人民群眾所喜聞樂見。

- rely on 依賴;依靠。例如:

You can't rely on the weather.

這天氣可靠不住。

- once in a while 有時;偶爾。例如:

He went to see them once in a while.

他有時去探望他們。

- laid-back 意思是「輕鬆、自在」,為俚語用法,be laid-back (about),這個詞組形容對某事的規定不嚴格。例如:

The dress code in many of Taiwan's mom-and-pop companies is laid-back.

臺灣許多家族式經營公司對衣著的規定並不嚴格。

- pull a fast one on 欺騙;耍花招。這詞組可指逗趣地耍花招,也可指惡意的欺騙,全憑上下文而定。為美式俚語。例如:

He tried to pull a fast one on us, but we caught on before he got away with it.

他想要欺騙我們,但在他陰謀得逞前我們就明白了。

# Unit 3 懂得適時讚美 Compliment People

## Fresh Expressions

I've got to hand it to you; you really did a good job.

我不得不稱讚你；你的確做得很好。

I should say my admiration for your skill is great.

我想說我對您的技術是十分欽佩的。

She performed on the balance beam with much grace.

她在平衡木上表演得非常優美。

Your necklace goes really well with your skin.

你的項鏈與你的皮膚真的很相配。

You're looking extremely dapper.

你看起來衣冠楚楚。

Her creative idea won her a lot of oohs and aahs.

她的創意為她贏得了一片讚嘆聲。

I must take my hat off to you for your good performance.

我要為您出色的演奏像您致敬。

He came through the examination with flying colors.

他考得非常好。

He has always had the means of making money.

在賺錢方面，他可有門道了。

I can't get over how good your English is.

我真不敢相信你的英文這麼好。

He has the gift of the gab.

他口才很好。

He is always ready to give the shirt off his back.

他對別人總是慷慨解囊。

## Interactive Dialogues

### Dialogue 1

A：The final report is exceptionally thorough and well done. I think that you have been come up with some interesting recommendations for the client.

A：最後的報告非常全面，做得很好。我認為你為客戶提出了一些不尋常的建議。

B：Well, I hope the client feels the same way!

B：嗯，我希望客戶有同樣的看法！

A：I am sure they will be pleased.

A：我非常肯定他們會滿意的。

B：You are so nice to say so.

B：你那麼說真是太好了。

A：I am really impressed with your presentation skills.

A：你做簡報的技巧讓我留下了深刻的印象。

B：Thank you. I have been working on it for several years.

B：謝謝。我已經做這方面的工作好幾年了。

A：Well, your time has been well spent!

A：嗯，工作的效果非常明顯！

B：Thanks, but I have to admit I am really good at bluffing!

B：謝謝，但我不得不承認自己滿擅長愚弄別人的！

**Notes**

- thorough 本意是「徹底的；完全的」，在本對話中意為「周密的；完善的」。例如：

  The doctor was very thorough in his examination of the sick child.

  醫生對生病的孩子進行了仔細的檢查。

- well done 不僅有「全熟的（牛排）」之意，在口語中還有一個很道地、很常用的意思，那就是「好！做得好！幹得好！」，用來表示讚許。

- feel the same way 有同感

- bluff 以假象欺騙；愚弄；嚇唬。例如：

  He bluffed me into believing that he was innocent.

  他裝模作樣騙我相信他是清白的。

## Dialogue 2

A：Look, Maggie. How pretty the tapestries are! These could be used to decorate our room.

A：看，麥琪。這些繡花毯太美啦！我們該買一些來裝飾我們的房間。

B：Oh, they're beautiful! (Looking at the price tags) But a little expensive.

B：哦，好漂亮！（看了看價格標籤）可是有點貴。

C：Artistic tapestry is the highest form of expression of the rug weaving art, an exquisite handicraft of superb artistry in typical Chinese style. Considering the fine craftsmanship they are worth much more.

C：藝術繡花毯是地毯編織藝術的最高階層，一件精緻的手工藝品，它是中國典型款式和藝術精品。單憑那精巧的技藝它們的價值就更高了。

A：I agree. Is this the marvelous landscape in Hangzhou? What a lovely tapestry! We are going to Hangzhou in two days, this tapestry is really impressive.

　　A：我同意。這不是美麗的杭州風景嗎？多麼美的繡花毯！我們打算兩天後去杭州，這件繡花毯真令人印象深刻。

　　B：I prefer to buy some embroidered tablecloths t o match the tapestry.

　　B：我想買一些與這繡花毯搭配的刺繡桌布。

　　C：Which do you prefer, the linen one, the figured dacron or the brocade?

　　C：您喜歡哪一種，是亞麻布的、有花紋的滌綸還是織錦緞的呢？

　　B：The brocade, please. How much is one piece?

　　B：請拿織錦緞的。一塊是多少錢？

　　C：One hundred Yuan.

　　C：100 元。

　　B：Too expensive. We bought a nice one last year, it only costs sixty Yuan.

　　B：太貴了。我們去年買了一塊好看的桌布，才 60 元。

　　C：I believe so, madam. Different things have different prices. May I show you something else?

　　C：我相信，夫人。不同的東西價格不同。我拿其它的給您看一下好嗎？

　　B：Sure. Well, this one is very nice. How fine the needlework it is!

　　B：當然。嗯，這塊好看。這刺繡多精巧啊！

　　C：And the price is not expensive, madam. It's sixty-eight Yuan.

　　C：夫人，價格也不貴。68 元。

　　B：Sixty Yuan, OK?

　　B：60 元，可以嗎？

C：(Says smilingly) This price is quite reasonable, madam. They are all first-class goods. We have price tags on each of them. Our shop holds a one-price policy. We are not allowed to change the price at will. One more thing, 68 is a lucky number in China, madam.

C：（微笑著說）夫人，這價格是合理的。這些商品都是上等的。每一件上面都有標價。我們商店堅持「不二價」。我們不允許隨意改變價格。還有，夫人，68 在中國是幸運數字。

B：Lucky number? Well, I don't believe in lucky number. (Begins to laugh) I think you are a good salesgirl.

B：幸運數字？嗯，我可不相信什麼幸運數字。（開始笑）我想你是個好銷售員。

C：Thank you, madam. I'm always at your service.

C：謝謝您，夫人。隨時為您服務。

B：Well, I'll take it.

B：好，我買了。

## Notes

- tapestry 花毯；繡帷；掛毯。例如：
  The walls of the banqueting hall were hung with tapestries.
  宴會廳的牆上掛著繡帷。
- price tag 價格標籤；標價；（物品的）價格
- exquisite handicraft 精美的工藝品。例如：
  Paper-cutting is a truly exquisite handicraft.
  剪紙真是精美的工藝品。

- artistry 藝術性；藝術效果

- craftsmanship 技巧；技術

- embroider 繡花；裝飾。例如：

  I embroidered wild flowers on the pillow.

  我在這枕頭上繡了野花。

- dacron【紡】達克龍；滌綸；滌綸線；滌綸織物

  brocade 錦緞；花緞；金線織花的錦緞

- needlework 女紅；縫紉；刺繡。例如：

  She spent the whole afternoon doing needlework.

  她用了整個下午做針線活。

- at will 任意；隨心所欲地。例如：

  He told us that we could wander around at will.

  他跟我們說我們可以隨意閒逛。

# Unit 4 請人幫忙 Asking for Help

## Fresh Expressions

Would you please let me a hand?

能幫個忙嗎？

Could you do me a big favor?

能否請你幫我個忙？

Can I help you with it?

讓我幫你忙好嗎？

May I ask a favor of you?

我可以請你幫個忙嗎？

I wonder if you could do me a favor?/May I venture to ask you for a favor?

不知您能否幫個忙？

May I bother you for a moment?

我可以打擾你一下嗎？

If you don't mind, I would like to borrow your pen.

如果你不介意，我想借用你的鋼筆。

Would you mind if I get a lift in your car, please?

請問你介意我搭你的車嗎？

Could you hand me the book, please?

你可以把書遞過來嗎？

Could I possibly use your bathroom?

我能用一下您的洗手間嗎？

I was wondering if you'd mind watching my house for me while I am away.

我在想，我不在家的時候，你能否幫我照看一下房子。

You might get me a gift for my son, if it isn't too much trouble.

如果不麻煩，你可以幫我兒子買個禮物。

Will you please help me download this file from the Internet?

請你幫我把這個文件從網路上下載下來好嗎？

I'd appreciate it if you could call me tonight.

若你今晚能打個電話給我，我將非常感激。

Could you spare me a few minutes, Mr. Li?

李先生，可以耽誤你幾分鐘嗎？

Could you do me a favor? My computer suffered from computer virus.

能幫幫我嗎？我電腦中毒了。

May I have the pleasure of your explaining it to me again?

我能再要求您解釋一下嗎？

I certainly didn't intend to cause you so much inconvenience.

我實在無意造成你這麼多的不便。

I really don't know what I would have done without your help.

真不知道沒有你的幫助我該怎麼辦。

I'm sorry to take up so much of your time.

真不好意思占用了你這麼久時間。

You are most kind. I wish I could repay you somehow for your kindness.

你太好心了。我希望能對你的好心有所回報。

## Interactive Dialogues

### Dialogue 1

A：John, could you do me a favor?

A：John, 幫我一個忙好嗎？

B：What's up?

B：什麼事？

A：Could you pick up David from Ford Company at the Taoyuan International Airport?

A：你能不能到桃園國際機場接一下福特公司的大衛先生？

B：Why don't you go?

B：你為什麼不去？

A：I'm supposed to pick him up at the airport, but the general manager called me last night. He said he couldn't come back to Taipei as schedule, so he asked me to attend this meeting for him.

A：我是應該去的，但是昨晚總經理打電話給我。他說他不能照計畫回臺北，所以他要我替他出席這個會議。

B：I see. I'll do it for you.

B：我明白了，我會替你去接他的。

A：I really appreciated your help. After you pick him up, you could take him to Wan Fu Hotel.

A：真謝謝你的幫助。接到他後，就帶他到萬福飯店。

B：Have you made the reservation?

B：你有預訂房間嗎？

A：Yes, I did. Please tell the front desk that they could put all expenses on our company's bill. You do the check-in for David, and then you have lunch with him. Tell him we are going to pick him up at 8:30 tomorrow morning in the lobby.

A：是的，我有。請告訴櫃檯，把所有費用記在公司的帳上。你幫大衛登記完後，就陪他吃午餐。告訴他我們明天早上 8：30 在大廳接他。

## Notes

- do sb. a favor 幫忙某人
- pick up 拿起；撿起；取（給）；用車接載（人）；好轉；改進；增加（速度）；（使）重新開始；繼續；獲得；學會
- front desk 櫃檯；總服務臺
- check-in 辦理入住手續。要給客人填寫入住表格，內容包括：姓名、性別、國籍、居住地、身分證（外國人護照）號碼、聯絡電話、入住日期天數、押金（由酒店填寫）。回押金單據及酒店房間鑰匙給客人。

■ lobby（劇場、旅館等的）大廳；門廊。例如：

The clocks in the lobby of this hotel set to standard time in different countries and are accurate.

該賓館大廳裡的鐘準確地照各國時間走。

## Dialogue 2

A：Bruce, can you give me a hand, please?

A：布魯斯，能幫個忙嗎？

B：Sure. What is it?

B：當然。什麼事？

A：This is my pay check, but I don't know some of the terms used here.

A：這是我的薪資支票，可是我不懂上面的一些術語。

B：OK, Let me have a look. You see, this pay check is divided into two parts by a line of dot. The upper half is a check and the lower half is a pay stub.

B：好，讓我看看。你看，這張薪資支票由一條線分成兩部分。上半部是支票，下半部是薪資單存根。

A：But what's the use of the pay stub?

A：但是薪資單存根有什麼用呢？

B：It's a record of your pay and deductions. You can check it to make sure that your pay is correct.

B：這是你薪資和扣款的紀錄。你可以檢查以確定你的薪資發放是否正確。

A：I see. Bruce, can you tell me what regular hour means?

A：我明白了。布魯斯，你能不能告訴我固定時間是什麼意思？

B：Of course. Regular hours refer to the hour you're required to work each week, while overtime hours refer to the extra hours you work besides regular hours.

B：當然可以。固定時間是每天規定你要工作的時間，而加班時間是規定時間以外的工作時間。

A：The regular pay is the pay for regular hours, and overtime pay is the pay for extra hours. Right?

A：那麼固定薪資就是固定時間的報酬，加班薪資就是加班時間的報酬，對嗎？

B：That's right. And gross pay is the total pay before deductions. We also call it total earnings.

B：對。毛薪資是扣款前的薪資。我們又稱其為總收入。

A：I guess net pay is the total pay after deductions. Is that correct?

A：我想淨薪資就是扣款以後的薪資。對嗎？

B：Yes. And it's also called take-home pay.

B：對。也叫實得薪資。

A：I see. Thank you, Bruce.

A：我懂了。謝謝你，布魯斯。

B：No problem. Remember to check the pay stub before you cash the check.

B：不客氣。兌現支票前記得核對一下薪資單存根。

### Notes

- give sb. a hand 助某人一臂之力；給某人幫助；幫某人一把
- pay check 薪資支票；公司簽發，能在指定金融機構兌現的支票

- pay stub 薪資存根;存檔的收據;用來核算簽發支票金額和應付的相關項目金額
- gross pay 薪資總額;稅前薪資
- total earnings 總收入
- take-home pay 扣稅後的實得薪資

# 就算不用考英文，也要繼續 speak English：

## 基本會話 × 搭訕起手式 × 求職用語 × 旅遊英文，掌握這幾大類常用英語，流利的對話比你想的還容易！

編　　著：翁哲維，朗悅

發 行 人：黃振庭

出 版 者：崧燁文化事業有限公司

發 行 者：崧燁文化事業有限公司

E-mail：sonbookservice@gmail.com

粉 絲 頁：https://www.facebook.com/
　　　　　sonbookss/

網　　址：https://sonbook.net/

地　　址：台北市中正區重慶南路一段六十一號八
　　　　　樓 815 室

Rm. 815, 8F., No.61, Sec. 1, Chongqing S. Rd.,
Zhongzheng Dist., Taipei City 100, Taiwan

電　　話：(02)2370-3310

傳　　真：(02)2388-1990

印　　刷：京峯彩色印刷有限公司（京峰數位）

律師顧問：廣華律師事務所 張珮琦律師

定　　價：350 元

發行日期：2023 年 02 月第一版

◎本書以 POD 印製

### 國家圖書館出版品預行編目資料

就算不用考英文，也要繼續 speak
English：基本會話 × 搭訕起手式
× 求職用語 × 旅遊英文，掌握這
幾大類常用英語，流利的對話比你
想的還容易！ / 翁哲維，朗悅編著．
-- 第一版 . -- 臺北市：崧燁文化事
業有限公司 , 2023.02
面；　公分
POD 版
ISBN 978-626-332-982-9( 平裝 )
1.CST: 英語 2.CST: 會話 3.CST: 讀
本
805.188　111019939

電子書購買

臉書